WING
&
CLAW

BEAST OF STONE

ALSO BY LINDA SUE PARK

NOVELS

Wing & Claw: Forest of Wonders

Wing & Claw: Cavern of Secrets

Seesaw Girl

The Kite Fighters

A Single Shard

When My Name Was Keoko

Project Mulberry

Archer's Quest

Keeping Score

The 39 Clues: Storm Warning

A Long Walk to Water

The 39 Clues: Trust No One

PICTURE BOOKS

The Firekeeper's Son

Mung-Mung

What Does Bunny See?

Yum! Yuck!

Tap Dancing on the Roof

Bee-bim Bop!

The Third Gift

Xander's Panda Party

Yaks Yak: Animal Word Pairs

LINDA SUE PARK

WING & CLAW

BEAST OF STONE

ILLUSTRATED BY
JAMES MADSEN

HARPER
An Imprint of HarperCollinsPublishers

Library of Congress Control Number: 2017954099
ISBN 978-0-06-232744-4

Typography by Joe Merkel
Map by Mike Schley
18 19 20 21 22   CG/LSCH   10 9 8 7 6 5 4 3 2 1
❖
First Edition

To Abby

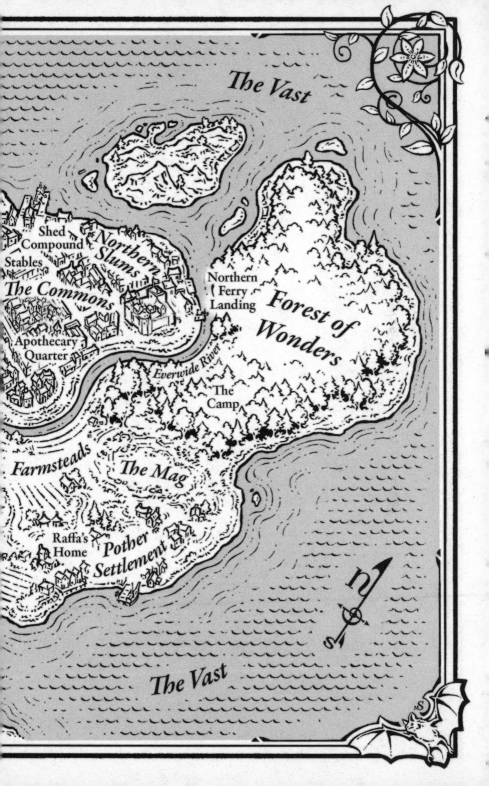

PART I

CHAPTER ONE

THE stripes of sunlight on the cell floor slowly narrowed. Raffa had been staring at them for what seemed like hours, willing them to disappear.

"Echo?" he called softly. "Time to look for Da."

The Garrison's stone walls were dank with mold and mildew, slimy in some places, furred with moss in others. Echo, a tiny bat, was hanging from a chink in the stone. He stretched his wings and chirped, "Look Da, where Da."

Raffa's father, Mohan, was also imprisoned somewhere in the Garrison. Ever since Echo had found Raffa in his cell three days earlier, Raffa had sent the bat out each evening to search for Mohan. But the prison was both vast and labyrinthine, and Echo had been unable to find him.

Raffa held out his forefinger, and Echo fluttered to perch there for a moment. "Try the daybirth side again," he whispered. Echo had already searched in every direction . . . but perhaps Mohan was being moved around? In any case, Raffa had no choice but to keep trying. "And then come right back, you hear?"

"You hear," Echo squeaked in response, and flew off.

As far as Raffa could tell, he was alone in this wing of the Garrison. On the two previous forays, Echo had returned and reported the presence of other prisoners elsewhere in the building, but no sighting of Mohan.

Raffa clutched at the bars and stared into the darkness. He heard the plink of water dripping into a puddle somewhere nearby. That was the only sound. Constructed of stone, the Garrison did not creak like a wooden building did.

The harder he listened, the thicker the silence became. *This time he'll find him. Third time lucky, right?*

The minutes stretched into hours. Raffa dozed off twice, even though he was standing; the second time, his head lolled, then jerked and hit the bars, a very rude awakening.

Finally he felt a slight movement in the air, followed by Echo landing on his sleeve.

"Ouch!" the bat said. During their early days together, Echo had alighted on Raffa's shoulder and pinched him. Raffa had exclaimed "Ouch!" Now Echo used the word to mean something like *"Landing!"*

Raffa retreated to the rear of the cell and turned his back to the bars. "What happened?" he asked in a loud whisper. The silence was so complete, he was worried that the guards overhead would be able to hear the slightest murmur. "Did you find him?"

"Where Da," Echo chirped sadly. "No Da."

Raffa swallowed a groan of disappointment. He stroked the bat's back with his fingertip, trying to comfort them both.

It had been months since Raffa had spoken to his father. They had been separated ever since Raffa had fled Gilden last fall. He had finally seen Da in, of all places, a courtroom, where both father and son had been accused of arson.

Making contact with Da would not, of course, get either of them out of the stone prison. But Echo's nightly searches had given Raffa hope, even if those hopes were repeatedly dashed.

In the morning, the rattle of keys woke Raffa as usual. Echo was safely hidden, hanging inside a crack between two stones in the darkest corner of the cell. As Raffa sat up and rubbed his eyes, a guard opened the cell door and put a wooden trencher on the floor. It would hold either a gluey porridge of oats (on the good days) or a piece of hard bread.

The guard was accompanied by a servient carrying two buckets. Raffa exchanged them for the buckets in his cell—one for water, the other for waste. He was careful to keep the buckets on opposite sides of the cell.

The long day began. When he first arrived at the Garrison, Raffa had spent much of the time curled up on the pile of rotted straw that served as bedding. Echo's arrival had changed that. Now gloom and despair were banished, as Raffa tried constantly to come up with plans for finding Da and escaping.

Echo slept for most of the day, which meant that Raffa still had no one to talk to for hours at a time. But what a difference it made, just to know that the bat was there, that he wasn't alone!

Raffa ate breakfast: half of whatever was in the trencher. He took great pains to divide the food exactly in two, and prided himself on the discipline it took not to gobble the whole lot. He put the trencher on the floor near the cell door, where the light was best. This was no guarantee against rats, but at least he could see them and chase them away whenever they got too close.

Housekeeping next. His only real task was to stir up the pile of straw bedding, in what was probably a vain attempt to help it dry out.

Then a series of exercises—whatever he could do despite his injured hand. Sit-ups, leg lifts, stretches, running in place. When he finished, he started all over again.

Afterwards, he prodded the muscles of his calves. *Getting stronger. Definitely.*

Rest time. Raffa sat on the floor leaning against the heavy iron bars of the door. He spent hours trying to think of a way to escape. The only chance was when the guard came in the morning. But he couldn't think of how to get past both the guard and the servient. What was he going to do, fling moldy straw at them?

When he felt his frustration mounting, he switched to thinking about apothecary, testing himself on botanicals and combinations and their uses. He did this for a long time, until it was bright enough for him to see well.

The cell, one of several along a corridor at the foot of a steep set of stairs, was a rough horseshoe shape, windowless. Narrow slits in the stairwell wall let in three shafts of afternoon sunlight.

Starting by the door, Raffa walked in a slow, careful spiral, looking at every inch of the stone floor. He walked the spiral again, beginning in the center, and then a third time in the opposite direction.

He never found anything except stray bits of straw and rat droppings. *But you never know,* he told himself doggedly.

Midafternoon was time for the second meal of the day. He ate slowly, making the food last as long as he could.

More apothecary and more exercises, until finally the light dimmed. Echo began to stir, and it was time to search for Da again.

Raffa decided not to repeat the mistake of getting his hopes up too high. Instead of standing at the cell door waiting for Echo to return, he lay down on the straw. *Get some sleep,* he told himself. *It will make the time go faster.*

When he woke, it was so dark that he wasn't sure at first whether his eyes were open.

"Ouch!" Echo said as he landed on Raffa's shoulder. "Da where."

Raffa shook his head, trying to clear away the sleep-fog. "It's okay, Echo," he said, his voice raspy. "You'll find him one of these nights. I know you will." But a shiver of panic chilled him. This was the fourth night. The Chancellor's vile cohort, Senior Jayney, had said that he would be back in "a few days." How many was a few?

"Find him," Echo said. "Da where."

Three or four is a few. Is five a few? Maybe I have one more night—

"Da where," Echo repeated.

Raffa blinked. He still couldn't see a thing. But Echo's words finally broke through his sleep-muddled thoughts: not "Where Da," but "Da where."

"Echo," he said, keeping his voice low and calm. "Did you find Da?"

"Find Da," Echo said. "Find Da where."

Raffa's heart thumped. *Stay calm. Make sure.* He knew from experience that Echo's speech was not always easy to understand.

"Is he far away, Echo?"

"Not far."

Raffa touched the little bat with his fingertip. "You did it, Echo! You found him!" It was hard to keep his voice to a whisper. He sat up and hit his fists together in silent exultation. "Where is he?"

"Birth peak birth peak," Echo began. "Fall peak star birth—"

"Oh, shakes," Raffa said, already lost trying to follow Echo's directions. The bat was using the words for the cardinal directions that Raffa had taught him: "daybirth" for east, "sunpeak" for south, "sunfall" for west, "nightstar" for north.

"Never mind that for now, Echo. Did you talk to him?"

"Talk Da."

"What did he say?"

"Raffa good?"

"Did he say anything else?"

No reply.

It would not be easy to use Echo as a messenger, with his limited speaking ability, but Raffa had nothing to write on or with, so he had no choice.

"Echo, would you please fly back and tell him that I'm fine, except for my hand?"

Beneath a soiled and stained makeshift bandage, a deep cut crossed his right palm. Whenever he made a fist, he felt a sharp pinch, which meant that there was probably a sliver of glass embedded in the cut. He wanted to let his father know about it—not as a complaint, but because he thought Mohan should be aware of everything that might be relevant to a possible escape attempt.

Raffa still had no idea how they could escape. He was hoping that his father would have a plan.

"Raffa good, hand no good," Echo said.

"Yes, that's perfect."

The next time Echo returned, he had a single-word message from Mohan.

"Hand?" Echo said. "Hand? Hand?"

It seemed that Mohan wanted to know what was wrong with Raffa's hand.

"Glass," Raffa said. "Echo, could you tell him 'glass'?"

"Grass," Echo said obligingly.

"No, not grass—*glass*."

"*Grass*."

Raffa groaned. When Echo had first spoken, he had used only words that bats would know, like *fly* and *wing* and *perch*, as well as the names of dozens of insects.

Since then, the bat had learned a good many words for "human" things. But Raffa had taught him those words by showing him the actual object—a rope, for example—and then repeating the word several times. Here in the cell, there was no way he could show Echo what glass was.

"Okay, let's try this. Tell Da 'glass' and 'pinch.'"

"Pinch? What pinch?"

"This. This is pinch." Raffa gave Echo's chest the gentlest of tweaks.

"Pinch Da?" Echo asked.

"Yes. Tell him 'glass pinch.'"

Even if Echo said "grass" instead of "glass," Raffa was hoping that Da would think things through. Injuring your hand on *grass* didn't make much sense. Maybe—probably—it was too much to expect that Da would guess that Raffa still had glass lodged in his hand. Still, Da would know that a cut, even a sore one, didn't "pinch," so if he thought about it long enough, he just might be able to decipher the message.

And Raffa had one other thing on his side: the invisible thread that so often bound the thoughts and minds of people who loved each other.

Please, Da, you can do it, you can figure it out. . . .

* * *

Again Echo returned, this time with a report as well as a message. "Pinch Da, say ouch."

"Oh! I hope you didn't pinch him too hard," Raffa said.

"Pinch *quiet*," Echo said.

"Echo good," Raffa said, and couldn't help smiling. Pinch quiet, such an Echo phrase.

"Da say, grass pinch now?"

"Wait—what?"

"Pinch now? Pinch now?"

Pinch now . . .

If Raffa's guess was correct, then it seemed that Da had indeed understood about the glass and was asking if it was still pinching him. Was he just worrying, the way parents did?

Or was there another reason for the question?

"Echo," Raffa said, "tell Da 'pinch now.' Say . . . say '*big* pinch now.'"

He was relieved that Echo didn't seem to mind flying back and forth. But at this rate, how would they ever be able to put together any kind of plan?

This time Echo delivered a message that Raffa found utterly baffling.

"Fire," Echo said. "Da say fire."

Fire?

Raffa frowned, thinking hard. Da had to be talking about the fire at the secret shed compound, which Raffa himself had set.

Chancellor Leeds, one of the highest-ranking officials in the Obsidian government, had ordered the capture of hundreds of wild animals. She was keeping them caged in a secret compound, and having them dosed with botanical infusions that made them docile and easy to train.

And was she training them to do the work of humans, as she had first claimed? No, teaching birds to drape napkins had been a ruse to cover her true intent: To attack people. Not enemies of Obsidia but *her own people.*

Since discovering the Chancellor's plot, Raffa had felt a terrible sense of guilt. One of the infusions being used to dose the animals was a combination *he* had developed. He hadn't meant for it to be used in such an evil way, but he still believed that he had a responsibility to do everything he could to stop the Chancellor.

So he had planned a secret trip to the shed compound, to release the animals. Part of the plan involved setting a fire, both to distract the guards and to ensure that the animals would run away from the city and toward freedom.

But the plan had failed almost completely. He had managed to release the animals from only two sheds. Hundreds of creatures were still imprisoned—creatures he would never be able to free, for now that the Chancellor had discovered his efforts, the compound would be even more heavily guarded than before.

Raffa shook his head, trying to shed those thoughts as if they were fleas. He admonished himself to concentrate. Why would Da mention the fire now?

Raffa kicked blindly at the pile of moldy straw. He lay down and began going over every detail he could remember, first of the fire and then of the trial.

No answer came to him. He tried again, starting from the beginning. This time around, he fell asleep.

And when he woke the next morning, he knew what Da was saying to him.

CHAPTER TWO

I T would not be easy. No, it was worse than that:
Raffa had no idea where to start.

*If only I had tweezers. . . . It would still hurt, but I'm
sure I could do it, even with my left hand.*

No tweezers—not even anything sharp.

Raffa sat on the pile of straw. He unwrapped the
bandage on his right hand. Then he pulled a straw from
the pile and used it to prod at the cut on his hand. It
hurt, and the straw bent uselessly.

He tried again with another straw. Same result, and
he cursed at the pain as he tossed the straw aside.

Next, he searched the cell again, knowing what he would find.

Nothing.

The triumph he had felt on deciphering Da's message was beginning to evaporate.

If Raffa was guessing correctly, Da wanted him to remove the sliver of glass . . . *and use it to start a fire.*

Raffa stared at his hand, which was curled in a loose fist. He clamped his lips together, then opened his hand and stretched out his fingers as hard and fast as he could.

"MMRRPHL!"

He stifled a scream as the pain brought immediate tears to his eyes. He blinked them away and looked down at his hand. An agonizing success: He had managed to reopen the cut, which had already begun to seep blood.

Raffa probed the cut with a tentative finger. *Is that— Yes, ouch OUCH—I can feel it, I can feel the glass!*

He made several tortured attempts to squeeze the glass out of the cut. It hurt so much that he could no longer blink away the tears; they rolled unimpeded down his cheeks and dripped from his chin.

Echo was dozing on the wall. He woke then, in the

way of animals able to sense the moods and feelings of the humans in their lives.

"Raffa no good?" he squeaked. He left the wall and flew to the perch necklace that Raffa wore—a twig tied to a leather thong. Hanging upside down on the twig, the bat looked up at his human. Echo's eyes, large in his tiny face, were black with a tinge of purple.

Raffa sniffled, torn between feeling sorry for himself and feeling ashamed of being a crybaby. Shoulders slumped, he looked down at Echo, hoping he would find comfort there, as he had so often in the past.

The bat hung from the twig effortlessly. Raffa had learned that bats were able to sleep hanging upside down because when they were relaxed, their claws closed tightly, instead of opening the way a human hand did. Echo's claws looked surprisingly like fingers, long and delicately curved and needle-sharp. . . .

Suddenly Raffa sat up straighter.

"Echo!" he said. "Can I borrow your claws?"

Echo closed his wings and wrapped them around his torso, as if he were going to sleep. This posture made it possible for Raffa to hold him by the lower part of his body. Raffa had explained what he wanted to attempt, and Echo had been puzzled but cooperative.

Now Echo had to extend his claws and splay them, which turned out to be a difficult feat for the little bat. Normally, when his wings were wrapped around him, his claws would be relaxed—meaning that they would be tightly clenched. Conversely, his claws were only extended when he was hunting, flying through the air with his wings outstretched. For Echo to close his wings *and* extend his claws at the same time seemed like the equivalent of that pat-your-head-and-rub-your-belly game—possible but not easy.

Besides which, Echo could only keep his claws extended for a few seconds at a time. I'll have to be quick, Raffa thought.

Then it occurred to him that there might be a way to use Echo's natural tendencies to advantage. After some hard thinking, Raffa made a small pile of straw and covered it with a piece of moss that he peeled off the wall.

"Okay, Echo," he said as he held the bat in his left hand, gently but firmly. "Claws out, please?"

Echo stretched his claws, and Raffa poked them through the moss into the straw. "Now relax!"

The bat's claws curled. Raffa gave a gentle upward tug, and Echo's claws emerged from the moss clutching a piece of straw.

It might work, it really might!

And it would hurt. A lot.

Raffa knew one thing about pain, from observing his parents treat hundreds of patients over the years. The *fear* of pain—the anticipation, the worry—was often more upsetting than the pain itself. So the trick was to get it over with quickly.

"We're going to try it for real now, Echo," he said. "Not straw this time, but glass. Are you ready?"

"You ready," Echo said.

Raffa sat cross-legged on the straw pile. He held Echo carefully in his left hand, then closed his eyes and breathed in deep through his nose.

"Claws out," he said, and opened his eyes.

As Echo stretched his claws, Raffa exhaled hard, from his mouth. At the same time, he plunged the claws on Echo's right wing into the cut on his hand.

The noise that came out of him was a strangled gargle; anything louder might have attracted the attention of the guards. Raffa blew out another hard puff of air to keep from screaming.

"Echo . . . relax," he panted, almost choking on the words.

Tears clouded his vision; he could no longer see. The pain in his hand was so terrible, it was as if he were holding a live coal. Blindly, he lifted Echo away from his hand, which was now bleeding profusely. The searing pain increased a hundredfold, which he would not have thought possible.

In that moment, he knew that if this didn't work, he would not be able to do it again.

Out of concern for Echo, Raffa kept his wits about him enough to put the bat down gently on the straw. Then he grabbed his right wrist and held it over his head, above his heart. He gasped between sobs, trying to get his breath back.

BREATHE! he screamed at himself inside his head. *Breathe—breathe—in—out—steady—steady* . . .

Blood was running down his wrist, but the flow was already beginning to slow. Meanwhile, Echo had unwrapped his wings and fluttered to perch on Raffa's shoulder. He clung to the knitted wool of Raffa's tunic with his left claw.

In his right, he was clutching something.

"Grass," Echo said proudly.

Raffa almost clapped in triumph—he stopped himself just in time. That would have hurt, he thought, looking at his hand ruefully. The success of the endeavor had muted some of the pain, but the cut was now a ragged mess. It needed a wash in pure water, a good poultice, and a clean bandage, none of which he had.

First things first. In a clear space on the floor, he placed four straws so they formed a square, a little frame. Then he cupped his hand below Echo's claw, and the bat released the sliver of glass.

It was a little longer than the top joint of his pinky finger, but narrower, tapering to an oblique point at one end. Raffa wiped it clean, then placed it carefully in the middle of the straw frame. He was taking no chances that he might lose it.

Next, he tore two strips from the bottom of his linen undershirt. "Sorry, Mam," he muttered. "I promise to mend it myself when—when I . . . whenever."

Hard to think that there might someday be a time when everyone could go back to ordinary things, like mending a torn undershirt.

He used one strip and most of the second as a bandage for his hand, the old one now too stained and smelly. He could not tie it as neatly as his friend Trixin had; still, now that the piece of glass had been removed, his hand felt a bit better.

Echo hung from the perch necklace, watching him for a while. Then the bat flapped his wings and flew to a dark corner where the wall met the ceiling. "Sleep," he said.

"Yes, you sleep, Echo. I'm sorry, but I'll need to wake you just after sunpeak, okay?"

Echo grumbled.

"Only for a little while, Echo. Then you can go back to sleep, I promise."

"Sunpeak *sleep*," Echo said.

Raffa could have sworn that the bat sounded a little petulant. Echo clearly thought that being awake with full sunlight blazing in your eyes was an absurd human habit.

Raffa tore the remaining piece of linen in two, and began shredding one of the halves. The threads had been woven finely, but not too tightly, to create a soft fabric for wearing against the skin. Unraveling the cloth was fiddly work, especially with his right hand hampered. It took some time for him to produce a small heap of linen threads.

Next step, more moss. He peeled several patches of

moss off the walls, tore the patches into smaller bits, and piled them up next to the threads. Then he broke up some pieces of straw and mixed them with the moss.

Raffa stood at the door and looked up at the slits in the stairwell wall. Narrow rectangles of sunlight slanted along the corridor floor. It would be a while yet, but the light would eventually reach his cell.

He couldn't remember exactly where the light had been the strongest the day before. For the moment, it didn't matter. He had one more task to see to, and this one would take some time.

He planned to position the shard of glass at the door, where the light entered the cell. But he knew he would never be able to hold the little sliver steady, and besides, no matter how he held it, his fingers would block a lot of the light. He had to figure out a way to wedge the piece of glass in place.

Raffa took up several straws and split them. Using a simple over-and-under method, he wove the split straws into a tiny mat. When the mat was a bit wider than one of the door's iron bars, he bent most of the remaining straws and broke them off. Then he made a second little mat. He tied the first mat to one of the iron bars and the second to the perpendicular bar.

He picked up the piece of glass and experimented. It took a few tries, but he finally managed it: With the pointed end pushed into the weave of one mat, and the side edge leaning against the other mat, the sliver stayed in place. He removed the glass, untied the mats, and stored everything safely.

Now all he needed was sunlight.

CHAPTER THREE

B E *ready,* he told himself.

If everything went as he hoped, he would escape from his cell and Echo would lead him to Da's cell, and they would both get away from the Garrison.

About five million things could prevent their escape. It was a tricky balance, trying to anticipate and plan for what might go wrong while not becoming completely disheartened by all the possible obstacles.

Time crawled. No matter how he occupied his mind, he could not stop himself from checking the sunlight's angle every few seconds. He tried deep breathing, and counting, and picturing himself and Da on the street outside the Garrison. Nothing calmed his twitching nerves.

When he could wait no longer, he went to the corner of the cell to wake his friend.

"Echo? Time to wake up."

No answer.

Despite the tension knotting his insides, Raffa smiled. He had seen the bat's head move. Echo was awake; he just wasn't ready to let Raffa know it.

"Echo, this won't take long, I promise. And then you can sleep as long as you want, okay?"

A grumpy click or two, and the bat fluttered down to the perch necklace.

"Wait near the door," Raffa said. "When I come out, I'll need you to lead me to Da."

"Wait, Da," Echo said.

"That's right. And, Echo, please don't fall asleep again. I'm going to come out running, and we'll need to move really fast."

"Sleep again."

"No, *don't* sleep again."

Echo clicked and flew off. For about the hundredth time, Raffa breathed silent thanks that the tiny wondrous creature was part of his life.

He returned to his vigil. At long last, the first corner of light was edging its way into the cell. Raffa made his best guess as to where the light would be the strongest and most constant, and he tied the little straw mats to the appropriate bars. Then he wedged the piece of glass into place.

What seemed like a lifetime later, a shaft of sunlight hit the glass and was refracted onto the floor of the cell, a bright spot of hope. Quickly Raffa placed a few of the linen threads directly on that spot—and held his breath, staring so hard that his eyes started to hurt.

Nothing.

He didn't move, didn't breathe, afraid that even a faint movement of air would snuff any spark. *Please let there not be any clouds in the sky today. . . .*

The light remained steady.

Was it—yes, a tiny wisp of smoke! It vanished so quickly that Raffa wondered if he had imagined it. But then there was another, and another, and now he could see the threads turning bright orange. Gently, slowly, he put more threads on top of the sparks.

His shoulder muscles were cramping, he was so tense! But at last he saw the orange threads merge into a minuscule tongue of flame, which reached out greedily for more fuel. He placed the remaining piece of linen fabric on the tiny fire and watched as the flames grew.

Now, in contrast to all the waiting he had been doing, he had to work fast. As soon as the piece of fabric was ablaze, Raffa sprinkled the fire with bits of moss and straw; the straw kept the fire alight while the moss smoked instead of burned. He fed the fire still more of the moss and straw combination, and the cell began to fill with smoke.

The moment of reckoning.

Raffa took one more deep breath.

"FIRE!" he screamed. "HELP! FIRE—"

He began coughing as hard as he could, hoping the coughs sounded convincing. Overhead, he heard the clomp of guard boots.

COUGH! COUGH COUGH COUGH!

He wasn't actually having any trouble breathing, but he was hoping that the guard on duty could hear his coughs. He lay on his side near the door, so he could see both the stairwell and the cell's interior. When the guard came down the stairs, Raffa closed his eyes, feigning unconsciousness.

"Wha's going on there?" the guard said. "HOY!" She stopped, turned, and went partway back up the stairs. "FIRE!" she shouted, presumably to her unseen colleagues. "FIRE HERE!"

Raffa opened his eyes a mere slit, so he could watch as she unlocked the cell door, opened it, and entered. She advanced into the cell, her attention on the smoky little fire.

Raffa stifled a gasp of surprise. *She had left the keys hanging in the lock.* It was an unbelievable bit of luck: He had thought he would have to try to snatch the keys from her hand.

"Faults and fissures!" she exclaimed, waving her hand to try to clear the smoke. She began stamping out the flames.

In a flash, Raffa was on his feet and out of the cell. He slammed the door shut, turned the key, and yanked it out of the lock. Then he was running down the corridor with Echo flapping overhead.

Behind him, the guard was cursing at the top of her lungs. Raffa knew he didn't have much time: Other guards would surely hear her shouts and be giving chase any moment now.

He followed Echo through the narrow corridor and past several empty cells. Echo swooped and turned; Raffa almost tripped as he tried to keep up. More turns—three, four, five—and he lost all sense of direction. *Where was Da's cell?*

Angry voices filled the corridor behind him. It sounded like an entire army of guards.

"Echo, where is he? Where's Da?" Raffa's voice was pitched high in panic.

"Where Da," Echo said, and alit on the bars of a cell door. "Here Da."

And there was Mohan, sitting on his pile of straw. His beard, usually trimmed, had grown out wildly, and his face looked gaunt and tired, but his eyes blazed with joy on seeing Raffa.

"Da!" Raffa cried out.

"Raffa!" Mohan jumped to his feet. "What are you doing here?"

Raffa was already trying keys in the lock. There were so many! At least a dozen of them, all nearly identical . . . Which was the right one?

His right hand injured and bandaged, his left hand slippery with sweat, he fumbled with the keys and dropped them, not once but twice. He wanted to scream in frustration. The sounds of the approaching guards grew louder.

"Raffa, you have to go," Mohan spoke quietly but

urgently, and reached through the bars to take the keys from him. "If I can get out, I will."

"No! I'm not leaving without you!"

Da grabbed Raffa's good hand and gave it a squeeze. "Raffa, I'll be fine—I promise. And we'll be together soon, but you have to leave. It's up to you now. You have to stop them. Find a man named Fitzer. He can help you."

"But Da—"

"NOW, RAFFA!" His father's voice snapped like the crack of a whip.

With a last anguished look over his shoulder, Raffa began running again.

"Out, Echo," he panted. "Get us out of here."

Raffa smothered a bellow of frustration. He had been so close to being with Da again! Leaving him behind made Raffa feel as if his heart were being torn partway out of his chest.

But there was no time to linger over regrets. Echo led him up a flight of stone steps and along yet another narrow corridor. Then the bat flew into what looked like a closet.

"Echo! What are you about?"

Even as Raffa spoke, he was following Echo into the small space. *I have to trust him—what choice do I have?*

With a quick glance, he saw shelves and wall pegs holding an assortment of items, including jugs, bowls, and mugs, presumably for the guards' meals. Why had Echo brought him here? They didn't have a second to spare—

At that moment, he saw Echo alight on an empty peg.

"Raffa rope?" Echo squeaked.

Hanging on the peg next to Echo were his rucksack and his rope!

Raffa snatched them off the peg and threw them over his shoulder; Echo had already left the room. As he came out, he saw a guard at the far end of the corridor.

"THERE HE IS! THIS WAY!" the guard roared.

Raffa grabbed a jug and hurled it as far as he could toward the guard; he followed it up with a bowl and another jug. All of them shattered into pieces; he hoped the shards of pottery would slow his pursuers at least a little. Then he dashed down the corridor after Echo.

Echo made another turn. Through the doorway ahead, Raffa could see the Garrison's courtyard. Whether by acci-dent or—more likely—Echo's design, they were about to emerge from the door nearest the gate.

Echo good, Raffa thought; he didn't have the breath to say it aloud.

Then another stroke of luck: Raffa heard a rusty metallic squeal he recognized. The gate was being opened!

A wagon had just made the turn off the street and was now blocking the entry. Raffa ran into the courtyard and pounded over the cobblestones toward the gatehouse. The guards pursuing him streamed out of the door.

Raffa was nearly at the gate—he could see the street beyond—but he was trapped between the guards and the wagon.

To his astonishment, all the guards came to an abrupt halt. He saw them looking toward the wagon, and swiveled his head to see what they were staring at.

The driver of the wagon was standing and holding up his hands in a "stop" gesture.

It was Jayney!

Raffa almost choked on his next breath. The last time he had seen Senior Jayney was in the cell four days earlier. Jayney, the Chancellor's second-in-command, was determined to recapture Roo, the giant golden bear.

He had made a cruel and terrible threat: If Raffa refused to reveal Roo's whereabouts—

Da! He said he'll torture Da until I tell him what he wants to know!

"He's mine," Jayney said to the guards, in his slow, deep voice. "No one else touches him."

Jayney crossed his arms over his broad chest and showed his teeth in what must have been a grin, although it looked more like a grimace. "Greetings, young Santana," he said. "Don't know how you got this far, but you'll go no farther. You and I, we have dealings today. And of course, your father is invited, too. Wouldn't dream of leaving him out."

Fear chilled Raffa's whole being. His legs felt as weak as straws, and the rest of his body began trembling violently. He envisioned Da on his knees, wracked by terrible pain . . . Da, broken and bleeding in agony . . .

A wave of hopelessness surged over Raffa. *I have to tell Jayney everything I know. If I do, maybe he'll leave Da alone. . . .*

Then he heard Da's voice in his mind.

"I'll be fine, I promise."

That was what Da had said. He didn't want Raffa to worry about him.

"*You have to stop them.*"

Them: the Chancellor, and Jayney, and all those who served under their command. Their plot to use animals against people had to be stopped, and Da was counting on him.

Echo had flown to the gate; Raffa saw him waiting there, hanging from the gate's framework. *If only I could fly like Echo, I could go right over—*

Raffa went very still as an idea came to him.

Not *over*. Over was impossible. But *under* . . .

Raffa lowered his head and raised his hands in a gesture of surrender. With a grunt of satisfaction, Jayney sat back down on the wagon seat and picked up the reins. Raffa took a quick breath and uttered a silent plea.

Then he did what he had always been told never to do around a horse: He ducked beneath it. The horse stamped in surprise, then shied and reared, a hoof coming within inches of Raffa's head.

Raffa collapsed to the ground and rolled under the wagon, which was now being jerked forward by the startled horse. Barely avoiding being crushed by the wheels, he kept rolling until he was out from under, which put him right at the open gate.

He scrambled to his feet. Echo flew to his sleeve and

hung on while he dashed into the street. He could hear the panicked whinnying of the horse and the roar of Jayney's curses as the guards tried to get past the wagon.

Faster! he screamed at himself. This was his chance to get away!

He wove through the traffic of pedestrians and push-carts. Up ahead he saw a street corner he recognized from the last time he had escaped from the Garrison. He turned into a small lane and slipped down a stair-well, which led to a cellar room where he and Trixin and Kuma had hidden before.

Only then did he collapse into a corner, feeling as though his heart and lungs were about to explode. It seemed to take forever before his pulse stopped its fren-zied hammering.

He had done it. He had escaped from the Garrison, and from Jayney as well.

CHAPTER FOUR

THE first thing Raffa did after catching his breath was to send Echo out on a mission.

"Echo, do you remember where Jimble lives?" Raffa said. Echo was still hanging on his sleeve. "We were there once, with his sisters and his baby brother—"

"Jimble friend," Echo said.

"Yes, that's right. Can you find his house again? I need you to go there and ask him to meet me here."

Echo clicked in annoyance. "Sleep," he said.

"Oh." Raffa's face reddened. He had forgotten his earlier promise to the bat.

He held out his forefinger and gently moved the bat

to hang there. "Echo, I know you want to sleep, and I didn't mean to break my word. But there are things we have to do. . . . If we don't, it will be really bad for a lot of creatures, and for humans, too."

Echo looked at him and blinked. "Raffa no good?"

Raffa was moved by Echo's obvious attempt to understand. "That's right. If we don't fix things, it could be no good for me. And for my family."

Echo gave a little chitter. Raffa stroked the soft fur on the bat's back. "It's not far from here, honest. It won't take you long, and afterwards—"

He hated the feeling of breaking a promise, letting both himself and Echo down, so he chose his words more carefully this time. "I—I'll do my best to see that you get some sleep."

"Echo go, Jimble come," the bat said, and flapped away.

Raffa had been right: It wasn't long before he heard footfalls on the steps. Echo flew in through the door and landed on the perch necklace.

"Ouch!" the bat said. "Not Jimble friend. Trixin friend."

Raffa heard Trixin's voice first: Even before she entered the room, she was already asking a question.

"However did you get out this time?" she said in that impatient tone he knew well. "Did you magic the guards again?"

It was just like her to start right in on things without the bother of a greeting.

He had told her before that apothecary was far more knowledge and skill than magic, but like many city dwellers, she still viewed the practice with awe and a little suspicion. "No magic," he said. "It's a long story—"

"—which we don't have time for," she said. "First, I need to tell you to be careful with that bat of yours."

Raffa looked down at Echo. "What's happened?"

"Rumors," Trixin said, "about a bat that can talk. I don't know who started them, but the Chancellor has heard about it. She's offering a reward to anyone who brings her the bat."

Raffa's hands shook as he put the perch necklace underneath his tunic. Echo was finally getting his well-earned sleep. *I need to get out of Gilden. Echo will be safer outside the city.*

"Come on, then. We have to hurry." Trixin strode past him to a door at the rear of the room; he jumped to his feet to follow.

"Where are we going?"

"The Chancellor is going to give a speech," Trixin said as she lit a candle. "It was announced yesterday morning, and it's been posted all over the city, and every family has to send at least one person to hear it. The guards have been in and out of people's homes all day."

A speech to the whole of Gilden?

"That sounds pretty important," Raffa said. "Has she ever done this before?"

Trixin shook her head. "It's usually the Advocate who gives the big speeches. But we weren't ever required to attend. And the guards—they're scaring people."

Raffa had never met the Advocate, holder of the highest office in Obsidia. His job was to represent the people. The Chancellor's was to execute the laws of the land.

Trixin began trotting. "We'd better hurry if we don't want to miss any of it."

They descended a steep set of stairs and entered a long passage. After a few turns, Raffa recognized where they were. Trixin's younger brother Jimble had once led him this way to show him how he could enter the Commons without having to go through the gate. They climbed a ladder that Raffa had used before. Now they were beneath a building just outside the Commons wall.

Trixin put a finger to her lips and pointed up. Raffa listened.

He could hear the tramp of feet and the buzz of voices. A great mass of voices: It was strange how he could sense the presence of hundreds of people overhead without seeing them. He pictured the Commons Green—a huge open space, roughly oval in shape, that served as the hub for the government buildings, walkways, shops, and elegant homes on its circumference. The Chancellor would be standing on the wide steps of Discussion Chamber, with the crowd before her filling every inch of the Green and spilling into the streets outside the Commons wall.

Raffa envisioned the Chancellor, tall and tan and silver-haired, a striking figure to all who saw her. But how would everyone be able to hear the speech?

Then Raffa heard a male voice, so loud and clear that its owner must have been almost directly overhead.

"Citizens of Obsidia, greetings! May your lives be solid and steady!"

Trixin leaned toward him. "They're using shouters," she explained.

Shouters? He knew how they worked, although he had never encountered them before. There would be dozens of shouters stationed throughout the vast crowd. The first shouters were positioned close enough to the Chancellor to hear every word she said. She would pause after a sentence or two; they would repeat her exact words, shouting them to their colleagues standing farther away. The second set of shouters would turn and repeat the words again, and on and on throughout the whole crowd in all directions, until every last person had heard.

"*Ours is a strong and proud land,*" the shouter said. "*We were able to rebuild after the Great Quake when all around us, so many others could not. A true demonstration of the superior strength and determination of our people!*"

Raffa frowned. It was disconcerting to hear a man's voice; he had to remind himself that these were actually the Chancellor's words. And he found himself thinking of his cousin, Garith, who was deaf.

I wish Garith were here. He wouldn't be able to hear the speech, but I could tell him what she's saying, and then we could talk it over. . . .

Because the Chancellor was twisting the truth. Obsidia had been able to rebuild after the Great Quake in part because of sheer luck: It had sustained relatively little damage compared with its neighbors. Beyond the Sudden Mountains, which had been thrust up overnight by the Quake, lay hundreds of miles of wasteland in every direction—untillable, uninhabitable. Obsidia had been spared such destruction, with the exception of an area called the Mag, a desolate place littered with eerie rock formations. If the lands around Obsidia now looked like the Mag, it was no wonder that no one had ever been able to rebuild there.

"As Chancellor, I take my responsibilities very seriously. Today I am announcing a program of new laws and acts that will not only protect our way of life but also improve the lives of our citizenry."

Raffa could hear a low buzz from the crowd, sounds of puzzlement that echoed his own reaction. What new laws was she talking about?

"Our first goal is to ensure better homes for our people. You are all aware that Gilden has two areas that are shameful eyesores, blots on our national pride. Those areas are going to be completely razed, and beautiful new structures will be erected in their stead."

The slums!

Raffa's stomach lurched. Several days earlier, he had

learned that there was to be some kind of campaign against the slums, but he didn't know exactly what the Chancellor had in mind. Now, it seemed, she was ready to execute her plans.

The shouter went on. "*Naturally, for such improvement to take place, those areas will have to be evacuated. Later today and tomorrow, residents will be receiving notice. Please cooperate with the authorities. Everyone must be prepared for removal in three days' time.*"

Raffa exchanged glances with Trixin. A frown line appeared between her eyebrows.

Almost at once, people began raising their voices.

"Removal? What does she mean by that?"

"Just temporary, right?"

"Of course temporary. She can't be saying forever—"

"*Those who receive official notice are required to prepare for departure,*" the shouter continued. "*Take only those belongings you can carry by hand. Guards will serve as escorts as far as the foothills of the Suddens.*"

Now the confusion in people's voices was mixed with anger. "The Suddens! We can't move there—how would we survive?" "What about my job?" "When can we come back?"

The crowd was no longer standing still. Raffa could hear thuds and creaks overhead; people were clearly becoming restless.

"*We will rid Obsidia of weakness and blight!*" the shouter bellowed. "*We will not stop until the land is free from all that prevents us from greatness!*"

Then he heard other shouts.

"GET OUT!"

"LAZY SLUMMERS!"

"AFTERS OUT!"

That last phrase quickly became a chant.

"AFTERS OUT! AFTERS OUT! AFTERS OUT!"

The chant was ugly and menacing. Chills shook Raffa to his very core.

Afters.

Obsidia's history was defined by the Great Quake, which had occurred more than two hundred years before Raffa was born. Afters were the people who had arrived in Obsidia during the years following the Quake. They had survived the Quake itself, but their homes and lands had been utterly destroyed. Then they had made a harrowing, arduous journey across a decimated continent and through the forbidding Sudden Mountains.

Afters were now part of Obsidian society and culture.

At the same time, they were proud of their own history and kept alive the stories of their struggles and triumphs. Raffa's father, Mohan, was descended from a family of Afters who had brought with them valuable plants and seeds from their former homes in the land of Zuelaca far to the south and west. Califer plants, source of one of the most important and widely used botanicals, were just one example of the countless contributions Afters had made to life in Obsidia.

Not everyone in Obsidia had welcomed the newcomers. Many Afters had ended up camping in two enclaves to the north and south of the city. Over the decades and generations, those camps had evolved into shantytown slums. Some families, including Raffa's, had eventually moved on and out. But the slums remained largely populated by descendants of the original Afters.

Da is an After. I'm half-After. The people shouting, they—they don't even know us. . . .

"Ears! Please, everyone, ears! We ask all citizens to allow the authorities to do their work without disruption."

The sound of the chanting faded, but Raffa could feel its menace lingering.

The shouter bellowed the Chancellor's closing lines.

"Thank you for your cooperation! We look forward to a new era of greatness, for Gilden and all of Obsidia!"

A smattering of applause was followed by the rhythmic thud of guard boots. Raffa guessed that they were forming up to ensure order among the now-unsettled crowd. He hoped no one would get hurt.

"I don't understand," Trixin said, her frown line deepening. "Why does everyone have to move out all at once? Surely they can't knock down every house at the same time. It's ridiculous."

While not an After, Trixin had grown up in the slums. Her family had recently moved to a better home near the Commons, but Raffa knew that she and her brother still had friends among the slum dwellers.

For a long moment, Raffa couldn't speak. He recalled his encounters with the Chancellor, and remembered especially her bouts of fury—when he and Kuma had slipped out of her grasp with Roo, and again in the courtroom. They had provided glimpses of her blind and unshakable conviction. He knew what the crowd overhead was only beginning to suspect.

She won't stop until every last After is out of Obsidia.

"It's—it's not about the houses," he said at last.

"What do you mean?"

"The Afters. She wants to get rid of all of us. My—my da's an After. His family was Zuelacan."

Trixin's eyes widened. "She never mentioned anything like that. And besides, she can't possibly mean people like your family."

He shook his head. "You said it yourself. If she really wanted to just clean up the slums, she wouldn't have to move everyone out—they could do it street by street. Or whatever. And she's already ordered attacks on other Afters, at Kuma's settlement, so it's not only the slums. And Garith told me that Jayney was talking about driving out all the Afters, remember?" It was all adding up to a horror he could never have imagined.

Trixin drew a long breath. "I'm not saying you're right about all that," she said slowly, unlike her usual impatient manner, "but it would probably be best for you to get out of Gilden. You heard her—there are going to be guards everywhere."

Raffa nodded. "But I need to talk to my mam first." After seeing her in the Deemers' Hall of Judgment and then wishing for her almost every moment that he was in the Garrison, he missed her more than ever. "Please, could you tell her to meet me here? As soon as she can."

"I'll try. But I don't always see her. She's out and

about a lot, treating patients. And you should think of somewhere else to meet. She won't know her way down here."

"My da," Raffa said. "I have to tell her that I saw him—"

He stopped, his throat lumping up. Why had he been so quake-brained with the keys? If only he had picked the right one straightaway, Da would be here now. Instead, he was still stuck in that horrid cell, and Raffa had no idea what to do next.

Then a tiny feather of memory tickled him. Da, telling him to get away . . .

"Find a man named Fitzer. He can help you."

Fitzer!

Before his imprisonment, Raffa had been trying to enter Gilden without guards seeing him. He had hidden himself in a wagon full of rotting compost, which had crossed the Everwide River by ferry. The driver had persuaded the guards at the ferry landing not to search the wagon, saying he was in a hurry. Raffa had overheard the guards say the driver's name: Fitzer.

Later, Raffa realized that Fitzer had known all along of his hidden presence and was helping him on his way. Neither of them had seen the other: Raffa had heard

Fitzer's voice but had no idea what he looked like.

With all the people in Gilden, how had Fitzer and Da met? Was it even the same person? And if it wasn't, how would Raffa find him?

CHAPTER FIVE

"OH!" Ratfa exclaimed in a sudden moment of comprehension. "Trixin, do you get deliveries of compost, for the plants in the glasshouses?"

"Of course," Trixin said. "How are you going to grow all those plants without compost?"

"Is it Fitzer? The driver who brings the compost?"

"Yes, Mannum Fitzer—that's him. Why?"

The mystery explained: Da had been staying in Gilden, at Uncle Ansel's apartment. He would have visited the glasshouses, maybe even done some work there, and that was how he would have met Fitzer. It was a coincidence that wasn't: Fitzer couldn't have known that the boy he helped was Mohan's son.

"He—um, he's a friend. Of the family." Raffa was mindful of Trixin's rather precarious position. She helped provide for her large family by working at the laboratory, a job she did not want to put at risk. She had agreed to tell him whatever she learned, but had adamantly stated that she did not want to know anything about what he was doing.

"Would you give him a message?" Raffa went on. "Ask him to meet me at the inn. The one near the ferry landing—he'll know what I mean. And if you see my mam, tell her that's where I'll be later today."

Trixin nodded. "This way, then," she said.

She led him through the passage until they reached a turning. "I'm going on straight here," she said. "You take the right, and you'll be walking a ways. Keep to the left every time. And you'll see some stairs, really steep ones—"

"I remember," he said. "Jimble took me that way before. I'll end up near the ferry, right?"

"Yes. . . . Oh, I almost forgot." She reached into her apron pocket and took out a napkin-wrapped parcel. "I figured you'd have had nothing to eat except Garrison gluck, and I remember my da telling me how awful it is."

She handed him the parcel. He unwrapped it to find an oatcake, split and buttered, and a handful of walnuts and dried apple slices. His mouth watered; in the excitement of the escape and the Chancellor's speech, he hadn't realized how hungry he was. He wolfed down half the oatcake in a single bite.

"My, that's a pretty sight," Trixin said, rolling her eyes.

Raffa chewed and swallowed. "It's not the first time you've given me food," he said. "I really— I mean, I don't know how to say thanks—"

"Don't be going all soggy on me," she said over her shoulder as she marched off.

And that was her good-bye.

Raffa climbed the steep stairs. At the top was a pair of cellar doors that opened into an alley behind the inn's storage sheds. He held his breath and listened but heard nothing. Cautiously he pushed up one of the wooden panels and peeped out through the crack.

No one was about. He clambered out, then sat down on the door frame in the shadows against the wall of one of the sheds. He pulled the leather rope out of his rucksack and began inspecting it, retying loose knots, doubling up frayed sections. It was work he really did need to do; it made him look like he had a reason for being there, and it also provided an excuse for him to keep his head down.

Guards would be searching for him after his escape. But it wasn't only the guards; Raffa couldn't help wondering about everyone he saw. Were they Afters? Or were they among those who had been chanting "AFTERS OUT!"?

Afters had come to Obsidia from lands all over the continent, which meant that you could not tell an After by his or her appearance. Some were fair, some dark like Kuma, and others every skin hue in between. The original settlers of Obsidia were mostly—but not all—fair-skinned. After two centuries of life together, there was hardly a family in the land without mixed blood somewhere in their lineage. Until the events of the last few weeks, Raffa had never wondered about whether people were Afters or not.

He didn't like wondering now.

The sheds had once held barrels of appletip; he saw the rotting remains of a few barrels and smelled traces of the beverage. He could also see a newer storage building closer to the inn itself; the sheds appeared to have fallen into disuse. He heard voices in the distance as travelers arrived and departed from the inn, but no one came near the sheds.

When the sun had lowered itself to just above the horizon, he felt a stirring under his tunic. He brought out the perch necklace as Echo stretched his wings.

"Skeeto," Echo said.

"Yes, Echo, I know you need to feed. But don't go too far, okay? And whatever you do, stay away from people. I'll whistle for you if I have to leave here."

The bat chirped in reply, and as Raffa watched him fly off, he felt a mix of emotions: joy at seeing Echo in his element, so graceful and at home in the air, and worry that this might be the time Echo did not return to him.

He didn't have long to fret, for soon he heard the sound of a wagon approaching. It looked like Fitzer's wagon, but Raffa wasn't taking any chances: He picked up the rope and ducked his head again. He would wait until the wagon passed him and then look up.

The sound of the horse's hoofs slowed, and the wagon creaked to a stop right in front of him.

"You'd be young Santana—Mohan's boy? Raffa, isn't it?"

Raffa raised his head and saw the wagon driver.

Sturdily built, with fair skin and reddish hair, Fitzer was wearing a brown tunic and trousers, boots, and a felt hat. He looked like a great many other working men—except for one thing.

The right side of his face was livid with a large purple skinstain, deeply scarred and pitted by acne. It made an ordinary face appear monstrous.

"Nothing happened, just born like this," Fitzer said in a voice both good-natured and resigned. Raffa was abashed to realize that he had been staring. He searched his mind for some way to atone, and blurted out the first thing that popped into his head.

"Me, too," he said.

It's true, he thought, surprised by his own words. *None of us can choose how we're born, or what we're born with.*

A shadow seemed to fall across Fitzer's brow as he studied Raffa's face, and Raffa began to worry. *Does he think I'm mocking him?*

No, it seemed that Fitzer liked what he saw, for the shadow vanished. "Too true, young Santana," he said. "Never heard it put that way before."

Raffa wasn't quite sure where to look. The skinstain darkened one side of Mannum Fitzer's face so that the other eye stood out. Raffa found himself wanting to look at that eye more as they talked. He had to remind himself to look at Fitzer's whole face.

"We've met before," Raffa said, "sort of."

"If you mean that your da has talked about you, sure upon certain," Fitzer said. "Don't think I ever met a man prouder of a son than he is."

Raffa's face grew warm with both surprise and pleasure; his father rarely praised him. He wondered what Da had said to Fitzer.

"Thank you, but that's not what I meant," Raffa said. "I owe you." Pause. "For a ride."

Fitzer cocked his head. "What do you—" Realization lit up his eyes. "Oh, shakes! That was you, was it?" He barked out a great guffaw of laughter. "You're very welcome!"

Raffa grinned. A whole long conversation had just taken place between them in only a few words.

Fitzer climbed down from the wagon. "Looks like we can talk here for a bit," he said. "I'll tell you what there is to tell."

After looping the reins around a post, Fitzer sat next to Raffa.

"First thing I have to say won't be easy to hear,"

Fitzer said. "I just came from seeing your mam. But I'm to take you to a safe place, and you're not to try to see her."

Raffa wanted to beat his fists on the wall and cry like a baby. *Why? Why can't I see her?* He blinked hard a few times. "I guess you'll be telling me the reason," he said, his lips stiff.

"I will," Fitzer said. "Your mam, she's been pothering ever since she came to Gilden in the fall, in between her trips to look for you. She's so good at it that all the Commoners want her. Even the high-ups like the Chancellor. So for a while now, your mam has had the run of the Commons, visiting all their homes and chatting with them, and even more than that, talking to their servients and tendants. I guess you could say that she's been working as kind of a spy."

Mam, a spy?

Raffa's mouth fell open, but just as quickly he snapped it shut. Why not? Hadn't Trixin agreed to do the same kind of thing, and her not even a grown-up yet?

And in that instant, Raffa understood Mam's behavior in the Hall of Deemers. She had not testified against Mohan, but she had also refused to bear witness on his behalf. And she had been sitting with Uncle Ansel, who had betrayed Raffa in more ways than one.

It's because she couldn't give away what she was doing. She had to stay in their good graces, Uncle Ansel's and the Chancellor's, so she could keep finding things out.

"Took a while, but eventually she pieced together what the Chancellor was planning. Nobody could believe it at first. But she and your da and other folks started making plans of their own."

"Oh!" Raffa felt as if he had just shed a coat made of stone. For months it had seemed to him that he and Garith and Kuma were alone in fighting the Chancellor. What a relief to know that his parents had joined the cause! At the same time, he found himself a little miffed that plans had been made about which he knew nothing. *Don't be silly,* he told himself firmly. *We couldn't have defeated her alone—we'll need all the help we can get.*

"Your mam found out about the move to evict the Afters from the slums more than a week ago," Fitzer said. "And since then, it's been all shakes and tremors, everybody getting ready in secret. Afters have been leaving the slums a few at a time. We didn't want the guards or anyone to know that we knew. And most of the rest are going to leave, too. Not in three days, and not to the Suddens, but tonight."

He shook his head regretfully. "There's some who are staying. They can't believe it, or don't want to. No convincing them to leave."

"Leave to go where?" Raffa asked.

"To the Forest. To hide and to get ready to fight."

At these words, Raffa felt a swash of eagerness and excitement.

The Forest of Wonders! It was many things to many people. To Gildeners, it was frightening and unknowable. Their ideas about the Forest were twisted with half truths and exaggerations, rumors and whispers of deadly plants and deadlier beasts. Those from the outlying farmsteads and settlements did not fear the Forest so much as they respected it, preferring to collect their firewood from less forbidding woodlands.

Raffa's friend Kuma was among the few who rejoiced in exploring the Forest alongside her friend Roo, the great golden bear. And the people who most loved the Forest were the apothecaries, like Raffa's family. Raffa had spent his whole life learning about Forest plants, some dangerous, others healing or healthful or delicious.

The Forest was one of his favorite places in the whole world, and he had not been there in more than half a year.

"Folks from the settlements have been in the Forest for a good week now, getting ready," Fitzer went on. "Nobody knows the Forest very well, except maybe you pothers, but the guards are mostly Gildeners, and they don't know it at all. It'll give us an advantage when the time comes."

When the time comes.

Fitzer explained still further. What Raffa's mother, Salima, had discovered confirmed his worst fears. The Chancellor, anticipating that there would be resistance to the evictions, had prepared the animals for a battle in the slums. Her earlier assertion that the animals were being trained to do the work of humans was merely a ruse to cover her actual intent. Mohan and Salima had allied themselves with a small group of others to lead the opposition, and the decision had been made to set up a base camp in the Forest.

"We're not going to let her chase the Afters out of Obsidia. It's as simple as that," Fitzer said. "Not without a fight, anyway."

Once again Raffa was shaken by a sense of guilt and

obligation. Not only had his use of a rare scarlet vine led to the dosing of the animals, but his actions since then had endangered his family and friends. He had to make up for that somehow.

The adults would shoulder the main burden of planning the resistance. *But there has to be something I can do. Something real.*

How could he help? What was he good at? Well, that was easy.

Apothecary.

Pothering is part of the problem. Maybe it can be part of the answer, too.

Raffa frowned, but it was a thoughtful frown, not a downcast one. He was thinking hard.

Thinking of ways to use apothecary to defeat the Chancellor.

CHAPTER SIX

FITZER went to the inn to buy bread and cheese, taking Raffa's waterskin to fill. While he was gone, Raffa summoned Echo. The bat landed and assumed his usual perch, upside down on the twig necklace that Raffa always wore.

Raffa was still preoccupied by everything Fitzer had told him. As usual, Echo seemed to sense his mood.

"Raffa no good," Echo said. "Eat Raffa good."

With a rueful smile, Raffa realized that Echo was right: The last thing he had eaten was Trixin's oatcake—tasty but not very filling. "Mannum Fitzer is bringing some food, Echo. Here he comes now."

"Raffa eat," the bat repeated.

"I will, I promise," Raffa said. "And Echo, I'm going to introduce you to Fitzer."

"Friend Fitzer?" Echo asked.

Raffa had debated keeping Echo hidden from Fitzer. But if Mohan thought Fitzer was solid, that was good enough for Raffa.

"Yes, friend," he replied. Then he had another thought. "That's a good idea, Echo. From now on, I don't want you to talk around other people unless I tell you they're a friend, okay?"

"Friend okay," Echo said.

Raffa introduced Echo to Fitzer as his pet bat, even though Echo wasn't really a pet.

Fitzer looked at the bat with interest. "Is that the one—does he really talk?" he asked.

"Friend Fitzer," Echo said, with impeccable timing.

Fitzer grinned. "Hello there."

"Did you know about him because of the reward?" Raffa asked.

"Yes. But even before that, there were rumors. Last fall, was it? Some guards claimed to have heard a talking bat. And then the rumors kind of died down for a while, but they started up again right after the trial."

That made sense. The first time Raffa escaped from the Garrison, Echo had been there. At least three guards had heard him speak. Then, at Mohan's trial, Raffa had become the center of attention, which would have started up the rumors again.

"I tried to keep it a secret even before the reward," Raffa said. "I was scared that someone might try to take him away from me."

Fitzer nodded sympathetically as Raffa tucked Echo down the front of his tunic.

"Let's eat," Fitzer said. He had brought something much nicer than ordinary bread: a hot pastry turnover filled with egg and cheese.

Raffa thought he had never tasted anything so delicious in his whole life. They ate quickly, and as Raffa licked his fingers, Fitzer took a look around to make sure they were still alone.

The wagon bed was empty except for a sheet of canvas that lined the bottom. Fitzer pulled aside the canvas, then slid open a trapdoor that had been cunningly cut and fitted. Beneath the wagon bed was space for at least two people. Not terribly comfortable, but tolerable for short journeys.

"Made it on your da's advice," Fitzer said. "I told

you, we've been taking Afters out of the slums for a few days now. Your turn."

Raffa climbed in and lay down, putting his waterskin within easy reach. The space in which he was hidden was a kind of wooden box. Like a coffin, he couldn't help thinking with a shudder.

Despite that ominous thought, he was asleep even before the wagon pulled out onto the road.

Raffa woke to a knock above his head.

"You awake?" Fitzer said. "We're nearly there."

The wagon rolled to a stop. Fitzer whistled, and Raffa heard an answering whistle. Fitzer released Raffa from the hiding place, then jumped down from the wagon.

It was well after sunfall. Raffa knew at once that they were near the Everwide River; he could smell its distinctive watery, muddy, reedy odor. Where exactly were they, and what were they doing here?

Echo poked his head out. "Eat skeeto," he said. "Eat skeeto eato skeeto keeto seeto—"

He was so hungry he couldn't keep his words straight. As much as Raffa wanted to keep the bat safe with him, he knew it wasn't fair to Echo. He had to let the bat hunt freely.

"Shusss, Echo. We're going to be with other people now. Don't talk, okay? And you can go ahead and feed, but please don't go too far. Come find me once in a while, so we can keep track of each other."

"Eat skeeto, find Raffa," Echo said, and flew off without waiting for a reply.

Raffa climbed down, stiff and clumsy after his cramped ride. He saw the bobbing light of a torch approaching.

"Once upon a time," Fitzer called softly.

"Happily ever Afters," came the answer.

Raffa peered through the darkness. In the wavering light, it was difficult to see—

"RAFFA!"

Someone flew at him and nearly knocked him down with a hug of greeting. "I thought you'd never get here!"

Raffa laughed as he embraced his enthusiastic welcomer. "Hoy, Jimble! I'm glad to see you, too."

Trixin's younger brother was ten years old, blond like his sister, with ceaseless energy and enthusiasm despite having to look after his three younger siblings all day, every day. During Raffa's time in Gilden, Jimble had helped out in ways both large and small, and had gotten his gang of friends to do the same. In only a few days, Raffa had become steadfast friends with both Jimble and Trixin.

"We came yesterday, me and the babies," Jimble said, "with Mannum Fitzer, in the wagon. This guard, she asked where were we going, and Mannum said he was taking us all on a picnic, and he'd organized it with me that I should get the twins to cry if there was any guards about, and Camma and Cassa set up with such howling that the guard couldn't wave us on quick enough!"

Raffa laughed again. He had met Jimble's siblings, and had no doubt that Camma and Cassa, the five-year-old twins, would have done their part with great zeal. Maybe baby Brid had joined in for good measure.

"Where are they now?" he asked.

"Asleep," Jimble said. "And Brid, too."

He gave Raffa's sleeve a little tug and leaned toward him. Raffa bent his head so Jimble could whisper in his ear.

"Is he here with you?"

Raffa tilted his head and looked up. "He's out there somewhere, feeding," he whispered back. Jimble had recently been introduced to Echo and was one of the few who had heard the bat speak.

"You know about the reward?" Jimble said, his eyes wide. "*Forty* coin!"

Raffa gaped. Forty coin was the amount a skilled laborer might make in a month. Echo represented the perfect intersection of the Chancellor's obsessions with both apothecary and animals. She's determined to get her hands on him, he thought with a shudder of fear. It was a dilemma he had faced before: his desire to keep Echo safe warring with his knowledge that the bat needed to be free to feed on the wing.

"We'll have to be extra-careful with him," he said slowly. "I'll try to give you a chance to talk to him later."

Jimble smiled and nodded and winked and put a finger to his lips all at the same time.

They had begun walking and were soon on a path that cut through tall reeds. Raffa recognized the green glow of lanterns and lightsticks made with the essence of phosphorescent fungi, a botanical invention of his mother's. This light was ideal for times when stealth was needed, as it illuminated the immediate area without shining too brightly. But the slum dwellers knew very little of apothecary; someone else had to have provided the essence. Mam, maybe? Or Garith?

The riverbank hummed with near-silent activity.

Raffa saw the water flowing to his right and knew that they were still on the Gilden side.

Then he spotted someone he recognized: Jimble's friend Davvis, tall and slim and dark-skinned. Raffa had met him in Gilden, when Davvis had helped Raffa lace a cartload of fish with antidote powder, part of an attempt to free the captive animals.

Davvis clapped hands with Raffa. "Everyone should be coming soon," Davvis said.

Raffa shook his head in puzzlement. Nearly the entire population of the slums—more than a thousand people—would be making their way here, using the underground passages and cover of darkness.

How in the name of the Quake would they get across the river without using the ferry?

CHAPTER SEVEN

D AVVIS grinned at Raffa's perplexed expression. "We've been making boats," he said. "Come see!"

Raffa recalled that Davvis and his family used to live in the northern slums, probably not far from the Vast, the ocean that surrounded the Obsidian peninsula. It made sense that they might have earned their living on the water.

"We made most of them downriver, away from Gilden, and brought them up last night," Davvis said. "We're finishing up a few more here. You can see how it's done."

Row after row of canoe-shaped boats were tied up along the edge of the river. As Raffa drew closer, he saw that they were made entirely of reeds.

Several activities were going on at once. A few people were cutting reeds. Others went back and forth delivering armfuls of reeds to the boat builders, who were working in groups of two or three.

The reeds were placed on the ground in a long pile. The two ends of the pile were tightly bound, with the middle spread out to form a rough boat shape. Then the reeds were tied together in bundles, and the bundles tied to each other to create the bottom and sides of the boat. Before Raffa's very eyes and in less time than he would have thought possible, a completely river-worthy boat was finished!

"So steady," he said, the highest compliment he could think of.

Davvis nodded. "My mam's in charge—you'll meet her later; her name's Quellin," he said. "Listen to this: She got into boat-building because she's scared to death of the water. She says that's why nobody builds a better boat than her."

A sharp whistle sounded. Every head turned toward the source of the sound. Whispers began to ripple through the night, passed from one person to the next until the eager words reached Raffa.

"It's them—they're here!"

Raffa held a lantern high to help light the way for the long straggle of people. In the lantern's greenish glow, he could see their tired faces, not a smile among them. Lost. Frightened. Angry, bewildered, sad.

During the deepest hour of the night, the slum dwellers had slipped into the underground passages, led by several youngsters, most of them friends of Jimble. They had emerged just beyond the apothecary quarter of Gilden, not far from the river. From there they were now making their way to the boats, which were positioned halfway between the two heavily guarded ferry landings.

The travelers had clearly been warned that silence was an imperative. With dozens upon dozens of people on the move, it was both impressive and eerie how little noise they made. Everyone was carrying something: baskets, grain bags, misshapen parcels filled with foodstuffs and other essentials. Adults and teens carried sleeping babies and toddlers. One little girl clutched a bedraggled cat.

At the riverbank, Davvis, Fitzer, and a few others

began directing and helping people into the boats. Oars were handed out, two to a boat; like the boats themselves, they were made of bound reeds. Raffa realized that the boat-building effort must have begun at least a few days earlier. A small but strong glow of pride warmed him, that it was his mother who had discovered the details of the Chancellor's plans and warned of its imminence.

Raffa's arm was getting tired of holding the lantern aloft. He switched hands, and the green glow wobbled momentarily. In that instant, he thought he saw a familiar face. He swung the lantern back and steadied it, searching the faces of those now walking past him.

"Garith?" he exclaimed, incredulous.

Even as Raffa uttered the name, he was already moving, knowing that Garith would not have heard him. Keeping the lantern above his head, he passed several people and tapped the shoulder of a tall boy in a leather tunic with a sack slung on his back.

The boy turned his head.

It was indeed Garith.

Raffa's thoughts tumbled and thumped. Garith had returned to Gilden to try to patch things up with his father, Ansel, who was in charge of making the apothecary combinations to dose the animals for the Chancellor. With an ache in his heart, Raffa realized that Garith's presence here meant that he must have given up on a reconciliation.

Garith stepped out of the flow of foot traffic. The two boys stared at each other for a long moment.

Raffa wasn't sure who moved first. An instant later, he and Garith were hugging each other, briefly but fiercely.

They stood with their hands on each other's shoulders. "I'm so glad you're here," Raffa said, and tapped his heart with one hand.

Garith nodded, then grinned. "Yeah, you are," he said. "Come on. I can't wait to get to the Forest."

The atmosphere was tense but orderly. Three or four people, depending on weight and size, boarded each boat and rowed across. After they disembarked on the far side, one person had to make the return journey to pick up another group of passengers.

Raffa and Garith held lanterns, offered a steadying arm, handed over parcels. Once, Raffa heard a splash when someone fell overboard, but whoever it was had been quickly hauled back in again. Otherwise, the crossing continued, slow and steady and without mishap.

As instructed, Echo found Raffa twice during the night. The third time, to Raffa's great relief, the bat returned to his usual roost on the perch necklace, heavier by several hundred mosquitoes.

The blackness of the sky was thinning to gray when Raffa heard a noise coming from beyond the top of the riverbank. For a moment he couldn't tell what it was, but then he recognized the sound of distant voices, combined with the thud of pounding feet.

People were running, and their voices were filled with fear.

Order immediately turned to disarray. The quiet line of passengers waiting to board the boats broke into knots and clumps of frightened people milling about—children crying, babies wailing, adults calling out in panic.

"What's happening?"

"What's all that noise?"

Raffa ran up the riverbank, struggling against the flow of people frantically pushing past him. At the top of the bank he saw more people running, and a man standing on a tall stump silhouetted against the daybirth sky.

"This way!" the man bellowed. "The boats are down here!"

"Mannum Fitzer!" Raffa shouted. "Can you see any-thing?"

"Go back, young Santana!" Fitzer shouted. "You have to get across! Hurry!"

Raffa hesitated, then pressed on toward Fitzer. He had to find out what was happening. Moments later he pulled himself up onto the stump.

"What are you doing?" Fitzer said. "I told you—"

"I'm going, I promise," Raffa said. "I just needed to know—"

Then they heard a shrill scream, followed by cries of alarm.

"RUN!"

"RUN, EVERYONE!"

"Dog—no—FOX! They're foxes!"

"Someone's down! Help!"

Raffa's blood chilled. Animals attacking . . . already! How had the guards found out about the river crossing? The Afters could have been spotted leaving the slums, something as simple as that.

He couldn't think about it now—he had to find who-ever was injured and do what he could to treat them. As he leaned forward to jump from the stump, he was jerked harshly and almost choked by his own collar: Fitzer had grabbed the back of his tunic and was holding him fast.

"Where do you think you're going?" Fitzer roared. He did not wait for an answer. "You get to a boat right this minute! NOW, or I'll drag you there myself!"

He spun around still holding on to Raffa, and dropped him off the other side of the stump, toward the river.

Raffa obeyed instantly; there was no arguing with Fitzer's fury. He ran back down the bank, slipping, stumbling, staggering. Boat after boat was being launched into the water, in complete chaos.

"RAFFA! RAFFA!"

It was Garith's voice, loud enough for Raffa to follow. Garith was standing waist-deep in the river, holding on to one of the boats. Raffa crashed through the water and flung himself into the boat, then grabbed Garith's arm to help haul him aboard. They each took an oar and began to paddle.

Raffa looked back to see Fitzer and Missum Quellin, Davvis's mam, helping load another boat with passengers. Where was Jimble? What about the twins and little baby Brid? And Jimble's chummers? Had they crossed in any of the earlier boats? Dozens of people were stranded, with more coming over the top of the bank every second. Raffa searched in vain for Jimble's blond head among the crowd.

He paddled a few times, then risked another glance behind him.

The ground at the top of the riverbank seemed to be . . . *moving*, as if it were a carpet being pushed over the edge. At that moment, the sun cleared the horizon, and Raffa could see plainly.

"No!" he cried out.

Scores of animals were now pouring down the bank. He saw the red fur of foxes, the sleek bodies of stoats, badgers striped black and white. The animals began attacking the people at the water's edge.

Between the shouts and cries, Raffa heard an unfamiliar thin whining sound and finally realized that it was coming from the guards.

Whistles. They're using some kind of whistle to command the animals.

Then he heard voices clearly calling out orders.

"RED, SPRING!"

"RED, SPRING!"

"SHARP, SNAP!

"FIERCE, LUNGE! FIERCE, LUNGE!"

Screams rent the air as people fled in every direction, some splashing into the river itself. Raffa saw a man trying to fend off a stoat that leapt at him repeatedly. A fox closed its jaws on a woman's shoulder. Another woman held a wailing child and kicked desperately at a menacing badger.

As Raffa stared at the turmoil, rigid with horror, guards appeared. They did not advance farther than the top of the bank but spaced themselves out and stood looking down on the chaos. They thrust their lancers viciously at anyone trying to climb back up the bank.

Raffa turned and saw Garith kneeling at the bow of the boat, paddling hard. Raffa reached out with his own oar to tap Garith on the shoulder.

"We have to go back!" Raffa shouted, gesturing wildly. "They need help!"

Garith shook his head just as wildly. "We have to get across—we can't risk getting caught!" he yelled. "PADDLE!"

Choking on a sob of frustration, Raffa spun around to face forward again and started paddling as fast as he could.

CHAPTER EIGHT

O N the far side of the Everwide, Raffa and Garith jumped out of the boat and hauled it ashore. Several other boats landed to either side of them. Fitzer, Davvis, and Missum Quellin were in the very last one.

"How many made it?" Missum Quellin asked as they joined Raffa and Garith on dry land.

Fitzer shook his head. "Hard to say. More than three-quarters, maybe? We'll know for sure upon certain when we get to the camp."

"What will happen to the rest of them?" Davvis was looking back toward the shore on the Gilden side. It was too far away to see anything, but Raffa shivered at the memory of what he had witnessed there.

Will they all be taken to the Garrison? Or will the guards force them to go straight to the foothills? In the chaos, families had surely been sundered—parents, bereft and in despair; children, wide-eyed with terror. The silence that followed Davvis's question was its answer.

Raffa saw the people who had arrived ahead of them hurrying up the riverbank and disappearing over the top. He hoped with all his heart that Jimble and his siblings were among the crowd.

"But how will they find their way?" he asked, knowing that most of the slum dwellers—maybe all of them—were unfamiliar with the Forest.

"Folks from the settlements were waiting here for them," Fitzer said. "A girl's leading them—a friend of yours, I believe."

"Kuma!" Raffa exclaimed, and immediately felt a little better. She was completely at home in the Forest.

And the slum dwellers had a head start: It would take the guards a while to reach the ferry landing so they could make the river crossing.

"She won't have been expecting us to cross," Fitzer said. Raffa knew he was talking about the Chancellor.

"It'll take her some time to come up with a plan. I'd say she'll send some guards in pursuit, but not many. Not to attack but to scout, figure out what we're up to."

Garith began digging through the sack he was carrying. He pulled out several smaller bags and handed them around. The bags contained some kind of powder.

Raffa untied his and gave the contents a quick sniff. "Throx?" he asked.

Garith nodded.

"What's that?" Quellin asked.

"It's a powder distilled from throx plants," Raffa said. "We use it as a stimulant—" He stopped and looked at Garith. "But why do we need it now?"

"Dogs," Garith said. He looked at Raffa expectantly.

Raffa stared at him for a moment, until his mind lit up with understanding.

"Oh! Shakes and tremors, that's brilliant!" He couldn't help a little hop of excitement as he spoke to the others. "Throx powder has an unusual quality: It numbs scent organs."

"*What* organs?" Davvis asked, in obvious puzzlement.

Raffa tapped his nose. "Your nose," he said. "Makes it so you can't smell. It's temporary, but it lasts for a while—an hour or two, at least. So we need to spread out along the bank, wherever the boats landed, and sprinkle the powder around as we walk."

"I still don't get it," Davvis said.

"The guards," Raffa replied. "If they try to track us, they'll most likely be using dogs. The dogs will inhale the powder, and—"

"And it'll numb their noses so they can't pick up our scent!" Davvis finished triumphantly.

"That *is* brilliant," Fitzer agreed. "If they don't find any scent trails into the Forest, perhaps they'll think we're headed for the settlements instead. In any case, it'll surely delay them, and we'll be needing every moment."

Raffa pointed a finger at Garith, and then tapped his own temple. "Your idea?"

Garith shrugged. "Yeah. Aunt Salima harvested the plants, because I wasn't allowed to go anywhere," he said, an edge of resentment in his voice. "And Uncle Mohan helped make the powder."

"Let's get to work," Fitzer said. He picked up a stick and drew a quick sketch in the damp sand, diagonal lines intersecting each other and making a sort of diamond pattern. "If we walk a grid like this, we'll be able to cover the most ground."

They spread out along the bank, staying within eye-shot of each other. Raffa climbed the bank, scattering powder as he went. There was enough throx to strew over an area thirty paces wide and nearly a quarter of a mile long.

As Raffa emptied the last of the throx from his bag, he heard Fitzer's voice, calling urgently. "Down, everyone!"

They were in scrubland between the river and the Forest. Raffa saw a tangle of cracklefruit shrubs and ducked beneath them. He sat hugging his knees, listening hard.

At first he heard what sounded almost like singing, faint and far away. The sounds were getting closer.

No, not singing.

Baying.

Dogs.

It seemed like no time at all before Raffa could hear voices. The shrubs around him were in spring bud, not full leaf. He felt so exposed that he might as well have been sitting out in the open.

"THIS WAY! OVER HERE!"

Were they coming toward him? Raffa stared as hard as he could in the direction of the voice.

Then a sharp bark—so close that he nearly jumped out of his boots! He swiveled his head and saw a dog off to the right, perhaps fifteen paces away, on a lead held by a guard.

Fear knotted his throat. In a moment of nonsensical instinct, he closed his eyes. *If I can't see them, maybe they won't see me. . . .*

"NO! *THIS* WAY! WHERE ARE YOU GOING?"

The voice was so close, it seemed he could almost feel the guard's breath.

Another voice, farther off: "FAULTS AND FIS-SURES, THAT'S THE WRONG WAY!"

"SEARCH, TRACKER! WHAT ARE YOU DOING? SEARCH!"

Raffa swallowed a squeak of surprise. *The dogs are confused! The throx is working!*

Now the guards began arguing with each other.

"My dog says this way!"

"Well, mine's pulling hard over here!"

"Arrow's more reliable than Tracker, and you know that's the truth!"

"Is not! Arrow couldn't find her way to a tree to pee!"

Raffa would have laughed aloud if he weren't trying so hard to stay quiet.

Guards and dogs crisscrossed the scrubland in confusion. Finally a guard who apparently outranked the others gave the order to head south—toward the settlements. Raffa gave a fervent, silent cheer. The throx powder had worked even better than he had hoped.

He waited until the guards' voices faded into silence, then began counting to one hundred. At seventy-three, he heard Fitzer calling.

"They're gone. Come on out, everyone. We're in the clear."

Raffa ducked out from beneath the shrubs and ran toward Garith. He whooped and tackled the taller boy to the ground, mock-pummeling him.

"You did it! It worked!" he crowed.

"Get off me, you quake-brain," Garith said, grinning.

Raffa pulled his cousin to his feet. The success of Garith's idea to use the throx powder had inspired him. As they clapped each other's hands in celebration, hope rose inside him—hope spiked with determination.

* * *

The glow wore off quickly during the hike to the Forest, for the memory of seeing people attacked by the animals remained vivid in Raffa's mind. Their fear had tainted the air like smoke.

He started walking faster. They entered the Forest and soon joined up with a path that he recognized. It led to a large clearing.

A place he had been to before.

Months earlier, he and Garith had made a trip to the Forest of Wonders. They had been appalled to discover an enormous clearing, created by the ruthless axing of dozens upon dozens of old-growth trees. The Forest had long been protected by government charter, because its plants were the source of such valuable botanicals. The cousins could not imagine who would commit such a terrible crime.

Later, Raffa deduced that it was the Chancellor herself who had ordered the desecration of the Forest. The clearing had been used as a base during the effort by her forces to capture hundreds of animals, most of which were either babies or pregnant mothers. Jayney and his complice, Trubb, had discovered that very young animals were the easiest to train.

Raffa was so preoccupied that he could not properly appreciate being in the Forest again. Normally, he would have been searching constantly for useful or unusual plants, and marveling at how the Forest had changed since his last visit. Now he hurried along the path, barely noticing his surroundings: It was yet another way that the small joys of life had been wrenched away ruthlessly by the Chancellor's schemes.

He found himself especially torn on entering the clearing. He hated this gaping wound in the Forest, and knew that the entire area around it had been stripped of much of its animal life. It would take years—decades—before it returned to anything like its natural state.

On the other hand, there was a grim satisfaction in the knowledge that what the Chancellor had made was now being used against her.

The clearing looked completely different from when he had last seen it. A tent village had been erected to serve as housing for the evacuated slum dwellers. The tents were makeshift, constructed of motley materials and, as a consequence, very colorful.

He made his way farther into the clearing. Near the center was a large open pavilion, which consisted of a canvas roof held up by poles. The space under the canvas was filled with rough benches and tables. Raffa guessed that both the poles and the furniture had been made using the felled trees. A stream ran near one edge of the clearing. A water station had been set up there, equipped with buckets and barrels. Next to the water station was a long fire pit, with big pots and kettles rigged to hang over the flames.

He was astounded. *Shakes, it's like a whole town!*

"Raffa!"

He turned and saw a small group of people heading toward him.

"Kuma!"

CHAPTER NINE

A SMILE split Raffa's face, and he saw that Kuma's smile was just as wide. He ran toward the pavilion to meet her.

"I'm so glad you're here!" "It's so good to see you!" they said at the same time.

In the next breath, "Where's Roo?" "Where's Echo?"

They laughed together, providing each other with at least a partial answer: The beloved animal friends were safe, wherever they were. As Kuma and Raffa hugged, Kuma put a protective hand over the small warm lump of Echo under Raffa's tunic. Garith caught up and hugged Kuma, too.

But Kuma grew sober almost immediately; there was no time for more catching up. "I'm to take you to the pother tent straightaway," she said.

Kuma led the boys to two tents side by side, not far from the stream. "This one is for pothering," she said, pointing to the tent on the left. She made a stirring gesture with her hands; Garith nodded in understanding. "The other one is for treating people who are wounded."

About a dozen people were lined up along the side of the treatment tent, some sitting on the ground. Although many of them must have been in pain, they were all quiet. Raffa looked over them quickly. He saw a man whose shoulder was bleeding, and another with bite and claw marks on his neck. A torn earlobe, lacerations to cheek and chin, more neck and shoulder wounds.

Raffa nodded at the patients in sympathy. His pother blood was quickening: He felt almost itchy to begin making combinations to help heal them.

Kuma lifted the tent flap so they could peek inside. There was a table for patients to sit or lie on. Another table held baskets containing stacks of fabric squares and rolled lengths of linen for bandages. Next to the baskets stood two large basins, one each of hot and cold water. Raffa was impressed again by what the settlers had accomplished in such a short time, but he couldn't help noting the improvised nature of everything he saw.

A young man sat on the table. Missum Yuli, whom Raffa had met at the settlement, was examining a wound on his neck. "You're here!" she exclaimed without stopping her work. "Kuma will tell you what we need. Sooner is better, please upon thank you!"

They left her to her work and went next door into the pother tent. Raffa turned to Kuma. "The fox," he said quietly.

"*Red, spring*," she replied.

They were both thinking of the fox they had found earlier, one of dozens of animals that had stormed Kuma's settlement. "*Red, spring*" had been the command for attack—to leap and bite at people's throats. That was why the injuries were almost all to the face, neck, and shoulder.

"You know animal bites," Kuma said, addressing both him and Garith. "They turn putrid easily, and can take a long time to heal. We can't afford to lose people to injury—as it is, we'll be well outnumbered. What we need is something that will speed up the healing."

Raffa glanced at Garith to make sure he was following along and saw his cousin's eyes light up.

"I've got something that might help," he said. He took yet another bag from his rucksack, opened it, and held it out toward Raffa.

At first glance, Raffa could see the color of the open bag's contents.

Red.

An intense, vivid red that almost seemed to be glowing.

Raffa let out a shout of near glee. Garith had brought with him powder made from the scarlet vine!

Garith put the bag of the scarlet-vine powder on the tabletop. Raffa stared at it for a moment, thinking.

Combinations made with the rare and elusive vine had proved to be miraculous, healing and curing sick and injured animals almost before his very eyes. But when the vine infusions were taken by mouth, the creatures had later suffered from dreadful side effects. No matter how dire the need, Raffa knew he could not yet give humans the vine infusion by mouth.

However, it was a different story with poultices, which were rubbed on the skin. Raffa had treated Echo and two baby raccoons with a vine poultice, and as far as he could tell, there had been no ill effects.

But he had not yet used the poultice on a person.

Anxious as he was to get the poultice to Missum Yuli, Raffa knew it could not be used until he was certain it was safe.

He flapped his hand to get Garith's attention. "The combination for slashes and lacerations," he said. "We're going to need a lot of it."

In addition to the vine powder, Garith had brought quantities of many other botanicals from the laboratory. This was an amazing gift—to have such variety and quality right from the start! Garith took charge of organizing these ingredients, while Kuma went off to fetch tools and equipment from the kitchen and supply tents.

Raffa hurried to the tent flap and called after her.

"Kuma, would you keep your eyes open for Jimble? Tell him we could use his help here. You'll know him when you see him—like Trixin shrank and turned into a boy."

She smiled at that, and waved her assent.

The cousins began their work. Raffa was conscious that they had to balance speed with caution; it was not easy to work both quickly and carefully. When they had made a large batch of the healing combination, he put a small amount into a mortar, then stirred in a spoonful of the scarlet-vine powder.

The grainy dust was incorporated into the paste, growing smoother with each turn of the pestle. Raffa felt his mind empty, in a good way, of all but the task at hand. The paste took on a faint red glow. A few more turns, and glow turned to glimmer. Raffa speeded up the rhythm, until a breathtaking flurry of sparkles and flashes danced throughout the paste.

Garith slapped the tabletop and grinned at Raffa, who grinned back and nodded. Garith understood, as perhaps only another pother could, the satisfaction of a beautifully made combination.

"How are you going to test it?" Garith asked.

Raffa glanced up from the mortar. "Actually, I have the perfect subject," he said. He held up his bandaged right hand. "Me."

Garith unwound Raffa's bandage and put it aside to be laundered. Then he fetched a clean one from Missum Yuli in the treatment tent.

Raffa washed his wound and dried it carefully. Part of him felt a sudden reluctance. He could not forget that another poultice made with the vine had caused a dangerous reaction. That was a different combination, he reminded himself. *This one was fine for Echo and the raccoons. It might not do anything wonderful, but it'll probably be perfectly harmless.*

He kept his body moving, hoping to dodge his doubt. He took a single breath, dipped his left forefinger into the paste, and quickly rubbed it onto his right hand.

"There," he said, his voice a little too loud. "Now we wait and see."

To his surprise, he sounded exactly like his father. How often had Mohan used the same words, cautioning him to patience?

He stared at his hand for a long moment. Nothing seemed to be happening. *But maybe that's a good thing. No pain or burning, like last time. Yes, definitely a good thing.* Trying to distract himself from his impatience, he worked with Garith to organize the tent space into some semblance of a pother laboratory.

A little while later, Kuma returned. She was carrying a bucket that contained a strainer, a pair of tongs, some hollow reeds, a paper of pins, and a few other items Raffa had asked for. She also had some welcome news.

"I found Jimble," she said.

Raffa hooted in delight and relief.

"He's helping set up a sort of nursery for the little ones," she said. "He'll be here as soon as he can."

A nursery? Raffa frowned.

"Kuma, do you know anything about what's going on?" he asked. "We're not here just to hide out, are we?" When the guards realized that the Afters were not at the settlements, it wouldn't take long before they widened the search to include the Forest. As a hiding place, the clearing was not the best choice: It was probably the only part of the Forest that some of the guards might know.

"The leadership council is in meetings all the time, talking about it," Kuma said. She named the council members: Haddie and Elson, her aunt and uncle; Mannum Fitzer; Davvis's mam, Missum Quellin, the boatbuilder; and Missum Abdul from the settlement. "And your da and mam, of course. Even though they're not here."

Raffa felt a pang of longing for his parents so keen that it made him gasp. He held his breath for a moment to keep from crying. Then he realized that his fists were tightly clenched. He looked down at his hands, trying to relax.

"Shakes and tremors!" he said. As his companions stared, he held out his right hand, knowing what he would see before he saw it.

He turned his hand palm up and opened his fingers wide.

The cut had already healed. The skin was firm, dry, and healthy, with only a faint line of pink for a scar.

CHAPTER TEN

RAFFA hustled the rest of the sample batch to Missum Yuli so she could begin using it right away.
Then he returned to the pother tent to begin working on
a larger quantity of the poultice.

"I can do it," Garith said. His expression was half-
defiant, half-pleading. "At least let me try."

He was talking about adding the vine to the combination himself. On a previous occasion, he had not been
able to draw any kind of sparkle or shine from the vine
botanical, which seemed to be the key to releasing its
remarkable powers.

Raffa hesitated. Garith was older than him by a year,

but he was acting as if Raffa was in charge. In the past, Garith had resented when Raffa tried to take the lead. *This will take some getting used to. . . .*

"No," he said at last, and met Garith's glare with one of his own. "We don't have time. Those people"—he pointed toward the treatment tent—"need the poultice *now*, so there can't be any 'trying.' You just have to *do* it."

He remembered Garith saying that his deafness had actually helped his apothecary skills, that he could now concentrate better. Well, here was his chance to prove it. He held his breath, wondering how Garith would respond to the challenge.

Garith nodded at him, and Raffa was heartened to see the determination in his cousin's eyes.

"I need to talk to the council," Raffa said. "Kuma, will you come with me? Garith, I hope Jimble will get here soon. He can help, and he'd like nothing better."

Raffa ducked out of the tent, not wanting to hover over his cousin as if he needed supervising. He hoped that his departure would send Garith the message that Raffa had confidence in him. He left without looking back, leaving behind a trail of thoughts. *Come on, Garith, you can do it, steady upon solid!*

* * *

Kuma led the way through the camp to her family's tent. As they walked, Raffa told her about using throx to lead the dogs astray.

"But surely it won't be long before they search the Forest," he said. "How do we know they're not on their way right now?"

"We've got watchers and runners," Kuma said, "at both ferry landings. We'll get word as soon as they start crossing over. But even before that, we'll know when they leave Gilden. Your mam has people helping her. Some of them send messenger pigeons, so there'll be plenty of warning."

Raffa nodded, reassured. He was especially glad to hear that his mother wasn't alone in her work.

"I want to ask what the council is planning," he said. "Because maybe I can think of ways to use apothecary to—to help."

He was on tricky ground here, and he knew it. The essence of the pother code was to heal, not harm. Raffa had already chosen several times to use apothecary for other ends. Once, he had temporarily blinded a guard using cappisum powder; on another occasion, he had given Jimble an infusion of mirberries to make him vomit on cue as a distraction. None of the effects had been permanent—but that wasn't the point. The point was, should he even be *thinking* of using apothecary as a battle tactic?

The question was part of a larger one—so large that Raffa sometimes felt that his head would burst from thinking about it. Was it an apothecary's duty to discover all the countless new ways that botanicals could be used? That was what the Chancellor and Uncle Ansel believed. Or should a pother's efforts be focused solely on healing, as Da had always preached?

Maybe there's another answer: Using apothecary for—for what's right. Whether that's healing people's bodies, or trying to stop unfairness. Even as this thought occurred to him, Raffa was aware that such choices were not always simple and straightforward. Still, it made him feel a little better to have thought of what might possibly become his own guideline.

The council members were sitting outside, on stumps arranged in a small circle. Quellin represented the slum dwellers. Haddie, Elson, and Missum Abdul were Afters who lived outside Gilden. Fitzer was there, too—not himself an After, but against the Chancellor's plans just the same.

As Raffa approached, he heard raised voices.

"—bow and arrow?"

"—not enough bowshooters—"

"—no other weapons, unless you count hoes and hammers—"

Frowning, Kuma put a hand on Raffa's arm and drew him back behind the corner of the tent, out of sight of the council. "They've been arguing a lot," she whispered. "Not at first. Last week, while we were setting up the camp, things went really well. But yesterday, right before all the Gildeners came, it was like everyone started getting tense."

Raffa noticed that she didn't say "slummers." She said "Gildeners." *Because that's what they are, even if the Chancellor and her—her supporters don't want to say so.*

The voices were growing more agitated.

"—blowpipes, for everyone else—"

"—even with blowpipes, it's not going to be enough!"

"That's not the point! Nothing we come up with will be enough!"

The last voice belonged to Elson, Kuma's uncle. Elson was usually calm, steady upon solid; on hearing his agitation, Raffa's shoulders grew tight with foreboding. *I*

*thought they would know what to do . . . that they'd
have it all figured out somehow.* He shook his head and
began walking back toward the pother tent, Kuma following him.

When they were out of earshot, he said, "It didn't
seem like a good time to talk to them."

She nodded, and he saw on her face the same worry
he was feeling. He forced himself to focus on something
other than his fears. "They're planning to use blowpipes . . . Have you heard anything more about that?"

"Yes. Some people have been cutting reeds to use as
pipes, and they've tried dried peas as ammunition. The
peas sting when they hit you, but they wouldn't stop anything bigger than a—a sparrow, maybe." Pause. "And
none of us are experienced with blowpipes."

Raffa's gloom deepened. How could they possibly
defeat the Chancellor? She had a huge force of guards
and weaponry. She had the animals, too. *And what do
we have? Hollow reeds and dried peas. There must be
something better. Here in the Forest . . .*

The gloom of uncertainty lifted from Raffa's shoulders, and was immediately replaced by a different kind
of load: the weight of responsibility. *I know the Forest*

better than all of these adults. I'm *the one who has to think of something.*

Immediately his father came to mind. Raffa had long struggled against Mohan for more freedom and independence in apothecary. *This is why. He was teaching me, but he was protecting me, too.*

The load of responsibility was heavy. And uncomfortable.

But he would choose it any day over hopelessness. And he recalled what Mohan had said to him at the Garrison. *He said that it's up to me, that I have to stop them. So he thinks I'm ready now.*

I can't let him down.

Back at the pother tent, he stepped inside and glanced at the worktable. He saw a large mortar filled with a new batch of vine poultice . . . which was properly quickened, snapping and popping with scarlet sparks.

He did it! It looks every bit as good as mine—better, even!

That was twice that Garith had succeeded with his apothecary combinations—first the throx powder and now the poultice. Raffa didn't want to make too big a tremor about it this time, which might imply surprise at Garith's achievement. But when their eyes met, Garith gave him a quick wink, then stuck out his tongue and crossed his eyes.

A welcome gladness warmed Raffa, dispelling some of the doubt. He made a pig nose back at Garith.

"We're running short of spineflower," Garith said. "Missum Yuli wants another batch for the patients who need re-treating."

"I'll go collect some," Raffa replied. In that moment, he realized that this was exactly what he needed: a little time in the Forest, gathering botanicals. It was one of his favorite activities, both soothing and stimulating; it would calm him down and help him think.

Only a few dozen paces out of the clearing, it was as if he were all alone in the Forest. The sight of the tents and the sounds of the people faded; no one else was about. Besides being exhausted and bewildered by their journey, the Gildeners would be wary of the mysterious Forest, and would almost certainly stay within the bounds of the clearing.

Raffa found a patch of spineflower almost immediately, recognizing the grayish-green foliage, even though the plant was not yet in bloom. He took a quick peek at Echo, fast asleep on the perch necklace, and couldn't help smiling. The little bat's wings looked like a neatly wrapped cape.

Harvesting the spineflower plants had exactly the effect he had hoped for. He fell into the familiar rhythm: choose, gather, move on, repeat. It didn't take long to fill a sack; still, when he was finished, he felt more refreshed than he had in weeks.

As he walked toward the clearing, the sack snagged on a shrub. He reached to free it, and—

"YOW!"

He snatched his hand back and shook it hard, as if it were on fire. "Touchrue," he muttered in disgust as he glared at the offending shrub.

Gildeners spoke in fear of Forest plants so vicious that they supposedly shot poisonous thorns at humans. Touchrue thorns were indeed noxious, coated with a sap that caused burning and blisters. There were other plants whose pods burst open, scattering seeds. Tales of the two kinds of plants had been conflated, giving birth to a falsehood. The touchrue bush hadn't shot its thorns at him. He knew better than to touch it, and chided himself for not looking first.

He examined the sore spot on his finger. Already a

blister was bubbling up beneath the reddened skin. It wasn't a serious reaction—he had jerked his hand away very quickly—but it was bothersome all the same. A hazeltine combination would soothe it; he wondered if Garith had any.

Without touching the shrub, he unsnagged the bag. Then he stared at a cluster of thorns for a long moment, not knowing quite why.

Darkness fell across his vision. He felt himself hurtling down a long, narrow tunnel before bursting out into the light.

He looked around in astonishment.

Nothing had changed. He was standing in the Forest next to a touchrue bush, holding a sack full of spineflower.

Raffa realized that he had just experienced one of his moments of intuition. Sometimes when he was working with botanicals, he knew *what* to do without being able to say quite *how* he knew. That uncanny ability had helped him excel at apothecary from a very young age. He could never predict when or how such moments would happen. Colors, sounds, light, or music—they were rarely direct flashes of knowledge. He always had to think about them, figure out what the secret parts of his mind were trying to tell him.

He was now learning how to best handle his intuition—to not rely on it exclusively but to use it combined with experience and observation and practice. It wasn't always easy.

Touchrue . . . it's about the touchrue. But why the tunnel? Touchrue . . . tunnel . . . touchrue in a tunnel . . .

"Ah!" Raffa couldn't help a shout. He took the time to carefully snip a twig full of thorns, wrapped it in a leaf, and put it in his rucksack. Then he started running back to the clearing, heading straight for the council circle.

CHAPTER ELEVEN

"AN idea . . . For the blowpipes."

Raffa stood in the middle of the circle, out of breath from his run. He had asked for and received permission to address the council members, who were still at their contentious meeting.

"Go ahead," Haddie said.

He reached into his rucksack and pulled out the leaf parcel. Unwrapping it gingerly, he displayed the thorns to those in the circle.

"These are touchrue thorns," he said. "Some of you know about touchrue—it's one of the plants that grows here in the Forest of Wonders but nowhere else. The thorns sting and burn when you touch them. You can see how long and skinny they are—they'll fit fine inside a reed. We can use them as ammunition for the blow-pipes."

He saw the adults exchange quick looks. Were they skeptical? Uncertain? He wasn't sure, but at least they were interested.

"The reaction is temporary. It goes away eventually, and it can be helped along by a hazeltine poultice. If we want to be sure that some of the guards are slowed down, I'm thinking that we should also soak the thorns in nettle essence. That will increase the chance of a painful reaction, and make it more likely to impede them."

The council had questions for him. Could enough thorns be harvested? How would people be able to store and load them without getting stung themselves? What if the guards were wearing heavy armor? How far could a thorn be blown from a reed with reasonable accuracy?

Raffa answered what he could. "Gloves—everyone would have to wear gloves." For other questions, practice and experimentation would be needed.

The council agreed to support the effort to try out the thorns as ammunition. The mood at the meeting had changed. While everyone still looked serious, the anger had dissipated.

Haddie spoke to the other council members. "Earlier we were discussing the animals. I'd like to propose that we include Raffa. He knows the animals better than any of us."

Elson looked apprehensive. "Doesn't seem right, Haddie, to put that kind of burden on a child."

Bristling a little, Raffa squared his shoulders and stood as tall as he could.

"I'm not asking him to come up with any answers," Haddie replied crisply. "Just to tell us his experiences."

"Then Kuma should come, too," Raffa said. "She's been with me almost every time I've seen the animals."

Raffa was pleased when the council agreed that he and Kuma were to return after sunpeak meal to share what they knew.

He made his way through the camp, thinking so hard that he walked right past the pother tent. Realizing his mistake, he backtracked and saw that there was no longer a queue of people awaiting treatment. A good sign, and he hoped it meant that Missum Yuli had been able to treat everyone successfully using Garith's poultice.

Garith, Kuma, and Jimble were tidying up inside the

pother tent. Raffa put the sack of spineflower on the table, opened it, and pulled out one of the plants he had harvested.

"Jimble, this is spineflower," he said. He showed Jimble how to strip the leaves gently, without bruising them, and sort them separately from the stems. "Would you get started? I need to talk to Garith and Kuma, but we won't be long."

"Take as long as you need," Jimble said. "That nursery tent—it's the best thing ever. The twins and Brid love it there, and I can stay here all day!"

Raffa sat next to Kuma on a log outside the tent, with Garith on a stump opposite them, so he could see both their faces.

"The council is going to ask me and Kuma to talk about our experiences with the animals," Raffa said. "But I want to do more than that. I'm hoping that the three of us can come up with some suggestions."

"Suggestions for what?" Garith asked.

"Using apothecary." Raffa went on to explain about the blowpipes and the touchrue thorns.

Garith grinned. "That's a great idea. I'll make the nettle essence. Jimble can help. I can already tell—he seems to have a real feel for pothering." A slight shrug.

"The only problem is, he talks all the time and he's always forgetting to look at me. I have to keep reminding him."

"Maybe have him stand across the worktable from you?" Raffa suggested. "Instead of side by side?"

Garith tapped his temple. "Should have thought of that myself. I'll try it."

"Okay, let's start at the beginning. The crows." Raffa looked at Kuma. She had been with him on two occasions when he had seen the trained crows.

"They went for our eyes," Kuma said, with a shudder, gesturing with two fingers.

The crows that attacked Raffa and Kuma the previous fall had been trained using scarecrows whose eye sockets held grapes. During the attack, the crows had rained repeated blows on their heads and shoulders. It was Roo the bear who had come to their aid: She had killed several crows and driven away the rest.

"Well, that's easy," Garith said. "Masks, for protection."

After some discussion, Raffa hit on the notion of using birchbark for masks. Kuma knew of a stand of parchment birches growing near the stream. It was quick work for Raffa to fetch several kerchief-size squares of bark. With Garith and Kuma looking on, he used his knife to cut two narrow rectangular slits in the bark, eye-width apart. Then he picked it up and held it in front of his face, curving the edges to form a mask.

"Creepy," Garith said. "Why didn't you make the eyeholes round instead? That would look more normal."

Raffa held the mask out and inspected it. "It *is* a little weird-looking," he admitted. "But I made them like that on purpose."

Kuma spoke up excitedly. "So you think—maybe the crows won't recognize those slits as eyes, and won't aim for them?"

"Pretty clever," Garith said. "What about a second set of holes? Higher up, like here"—he pointed at the hairline on the mask—"and make them rounder. So the crows will aim for those instead."

That idea was greeted with enthusiasm; Raffa quickly added a second set of eyeholes to the mask. They made several more masks, refining the design each time; by the time they finished, the supper gong was clanging.

They stood in line by the fire pit, each receiving a ladleful of mush, another of lentil stew, and a piece of bread for scooping. The aromas of the hot food made Raffa's knees weak. At the table, he shoveled and gobbled, his manners completely vanquished by hunger.

Raffa held up a mask while Kuma handed out the others to the council members. He had already described the crow attack, and the reasoning behind using the masks.

"Hmm," said Missum Quellin. "I don't suppose the masks will do any harm. But to be honest, I'm more worried about the other creatures."

"Let's show the masks to the squad leaders," Fitzer suggested. "They can see to it that everyone makes their own."

"Good," Haddie said. "Now, Raffa, tell us what you know about the foxes and the stoats." She went on to say that the council had already discussed the attack at the settlement; she and Elson had witnessed it firsthand.

Taken aback that the masks had garnered so little attention, Raffa took a moment to gather his thoughts. He started by describing what he had seen at the riverbank. "The foxes and the stoats both attack by jumping," he said. "They snap and tear with their teeth, and there have been claw injuries, too. It's unusual for foxes to hunt in packs, but that's what these have been trained to do."

He continued, "At the settlement, they attacked animals—the foxes went for the sheep and the stoats for the chickens. But at the river, they attacked people."

"Stoats are so small," Missum Abdul pointed out. "Could they really do serious damage to a full-grown person?"

"They're small, but they're vicious, and their teeth are really sharp," Raffa replied. He swallowed. "The injuries we saw here—they're the people who got away. We don't know anything about the ones who were hurt worse—and couldn't get across."

A sober silence.

"We have to face facts," Elson said at last. "We don't have anywhere near enough bowshooters. The blow-pipes might slow down both guards and animals, but we can't expect more than that. We're going to need another strategy."

"Poisoned bait," Fitzer said in a weary voice that implied he had said it before—several times.

Everyone spoke at once. "Not with the bait again—" "We've been over this!" "We can't count on it—"

A piercing whistle cut through the jumble of voices.

Raffa was startled twice over—once by the sound itself and then when he realized that it was Kuma who had whistled.

She stood an arm's length from him. Every face turned toward her. She took a deep breath. When she spoke, her voice was so tight that she seemed to be forcing the words out one by one.

"I've heard talk of—of bowshooters. And poison. I might be wrong, but I don't think so." She stared at her aunt and uncle in turn. "You're talking about killing them. The animals. Or at least hurting them badly."

No one answered. Kuma's eyes were bright with rage.

"Don't you realize how unfair that is? Those animals—they're like slaves. They're being forced to do things against their nature! We should be talking about *rescuing* them, not killing them!"

Now she was shaking, and near tears. Elson stood and put his arm around her shoulders.

"Kuma, we talked about that in earlier meetings. None of us want to do it, but it's self-defense. What choice do we have?"

Haddie spoke gently. "Our first priority has to be people, Kuma."

"I'm not saying put the animals first," Kuma said,

her voice calmer but still fierce. "But they—she just—she does whatever she wants, without respecting anything. The Afters, the animals, the Forest—it's all the same *wrongness*. We can't fight just one part of it. We have to fight it all."

Raffa's eyes were wide. He thought of Kuma as shy and reticent, but here she was speaking her mind to a group of adults. It's because she cares so much, he thought. *Defeating the Chancellor is more important to her than—than being shy is.*

"You're right," Fitzer said. "We *have* focused more on the guards than the animals. It's why we asked you to join us here. We were hoping that information about the animals would help us come up with some new ideas. But—" He looked around the circle and shook his head.

"So what *are* you planning to do about the guards?" Raffa asked.

The adults exchanged glances. "Might as well tell them," Quellin said, "seeing as we'll be announcing it to the whole camp soon."

Haddie nodded in agreement. "You already know that we'll be outnumbered," she said to Raffa and Kuma, "and that they'll have weapons. We're not even thinking of trying to defeat them in the usual sense of the word."

But then how—

Fitzer spoke next. "Some of the guards are Afters. Or at least part-After. They're our neighbors—even friends or family. We see them at the market, on the street, at the ferry. We're planning to draw them here, to the clearing, as many as we can. But we won't fight them. We'll surrender, but as we do, we'll talk to them. We'll try to convince them to put down their arms and come over to our side."

Kuma raised her head in excitement. "If it works, maybe nobody will get hurt."

Haddie coughed a little. "That's what we're hoping," she said.

Something in her voice made Raffa glance at her, and then at the other council members. What he saw made his stomach clench. Fitzer, Elson, Haddie—their eyes were full of doubt and sadness.

They don't believe it will work. . . . And they don't have another plan.

CHAPTER TWELVE

As Raffa tried to digest this bleak realization, he heard shouts coming from the direction of the entrance to the clearing.

"HORSE AND RIDER! HORSE AND RIDER!"

The council members jumped to their feet.

"Stay here," Haddie said to Kuma.

Once the adults had all rushed off, Raffa and Kuma exchanged glances, and began running too. When they drew near the entrance, they saw that the path into the clearing was blocked by a group of people holding improvised weapons—pitchforks, scythes, hoes. Raffa could hear hoofbeats, which grew louder and then slowed as the rider approached.

The horse was a majestic animal, a chestnut with a white blaze and white socks on his forelegs. The rider was a teenaged boy, perhaps sixteen or seventeen years old, dark-haired and olive-skinned, whose fine clothing and beautiful saddle marked him on sight as a Commoner.

"HOY!" the man next to Elson shouted, waving a scythe in the air. "Stop where you are! Who are you and what's your business here?"

The rider immediately reined his horse to a halt. He raised a hand in the air. "Aren't you going to say 'Once upon a time'?" he asked.

Surprise rippled through the group.

"He knows the code." "Who could have told him?" "Why would a Commoner have the code?"

The rider raised his voice a little. "All right, then, I'll do it myself. You say 'Once upon a time,' and I say 'Happily ever Afters.'"

Still no one moved, and Raffa felt the tension rising. *If a Commoner knows the code, does that mean someone has betrayed us? Does the Chancellor already know we're here?* He could see his own doubts reflected in the grim faces of those blocking the path.

The rider must have sensed it, too, for he spoke again.

"I have a message," he called, "for the leadership council, from Senior Salima Vale."

Raffa gasped and started forward. Fitzer, standing next to him, clamped a hand on his shoulder and held him back.

"Wait," Fitzer growled low. "It could be a trick."

"So you know the code," the scythe-man said. "Do you have any other way to prove that you're solid?"

The rider looked from face to face, clearly nervous. But when he spoke, his voice was steady. "She said that her son would be here and could confirm this: The last time he saw her, she was wearing a yellow tunic. He helped her dye it, using onion skins."

Raffa saw both Elson and Fitzer looking at him. He nodded: What the rider had said was true.

"Good lad." Elson clapped his shoulder, then strode forward, calling out, "Dismount, rider, and tell us who you are."

At a gesture from Haddie, the man with the scythe searched the rider for weapons, finding none. The council then ordered everyone else back to their work.

"We'll give a full accounting at camp meeting tonight," Quellin promised. The crowd melted away, some people still looking back in curiosity. Both Raffa and Kuma stayed where they were. Haddie and Elson exchanged glances over their heads, but said nothing.

The council formed a semicircle around the horse, far enough away not to spook the animal. The young man stood with one hand on the horse's bridle.

"My name is Callian," he said. "Callian Marshall."

"Marshall!" Fitzer said in surprise. "You're the Advocate's son?"

The Advocate! Raffa stared, his mouth agape. *Advocate Marshall—that's his name. This is his son?*

Raffa burrowed through his memory for what he knew about the Advocate's family. *His wife—she died years ago. When I was much younger. And they had a boy, and he was an only child, wasn't he?*

Raffa saw surprise flash across Callian's face as he noticed Fitzer's skinstain, but he covered his reaction quickly.

"Yes," Callian replied. "I'm here because—because Senior Salima persuaded me to leave Gilden. My da, the Advocate . . . Something's not right with him. She's trying to figure it out, and she was afraid that I'd be next, so I—"

"Hoy," Elson said. "Next for what?"

Callian swallowed, and for the first time, Raffa thought he looked more frightened than nervous. "We think my da's being poisoned."

Sharp gasps all around, and in that moment Raffa felt the mood of the group shift, from uncertainty to sympathy. Elson came forward and raised his hand to match palms with Callian.

"Steady yourself, son," he said. "You're among friends now."

Callian's face tightened. "I don't know exactly what's happening, or when it started," he said. "I blame myself for not noticing sooner."

He explained that over the past few months his father had become more and more withdrawn, staying in his quarters much of the time and neglecting his official duties. "Whenever I saw him, he seemed really distracted, not himself at all. His eyes don't focus right, and when he talks, he can't seem to finish a sentence. He's all sort of vague and—and stupid."

Raffa remembered seeing Advocate Marshall at

Mohan's trial. In the midst of a commotion, the Advocate had appeared oddly detached.

"I talked to his staff about it," Callian went on, "but they brushed me off. So finally I went to Senior Salima."

Salima had explained to him that several weeks earlier she had been asked by the Advocate's personal health tendant to prepare quantities of two different infusions. One was a sleep aid, to be taken at night, the other a calmative without sedative qualities for daytime.

"She thinks he's being given them together," Callian said. "I searched his quarters, but I didn't find the infusions. His tendants must be keeping them."

Raffa sucked in his breath. He knew the infusions that his mother would most likely have prepared—and that it was dangerous to take them both at the same time. The result would be symptoms like those being suffered by the Advocate.

"Senior Salima said that if someone *is* trying to poison my father, then I might not be safe, either. I didn't want to go—I wanted to stay with him. But there's another reason I left. The Chancellor had all the messenger pigeons confiscated, so this was the best way to get word to you."

He shook his head. "What the Chancellor's been doing—the Afters and the animals and everything—Senior Salima told me that, too. I didn't know about any of it, and I'm sure my da doesn't, either."

"The Advocate's being poisoned to get him out of the way?" Quellin asked. "So he won't stop the Chancellor's plans?"

"Well, yes," Callian said, "most of all because the Advocate commands the guards. They're only following the Chancellor's orders now because my father's not around. He's under watch every minute, night and day. Senior Salima is working on a plan to get him away from his guards, so she can fix whatever's wrong with him and get him back to himself. Then he'll take command of the guards again. The Chancellor can't possibly succeed without them."

"Wait." Haddie put her hand up, although no one was moving. Raffa saw that beneath her kerchief her brow was furrowed deeply. When she looked up, her face was filled with such excitement that it seemed he could almost see sparks in her eyes.

"That's it," she said. "He's just given us the answer. We have to get word to Salima. She needs to cure the

Advocate of—of whatever's ailing him, and then bring him *here*. He's the one who can order the guards to stop what they're doing!"

Fitzer's voice was equally excited. "She might not even need to get him here. Couldn't he just do it from Gilden—give orders from there?"

"We can't trust that the orders will go through," Callian said slowly. "Nobody knows for sure any-more who's with the Chancellor and who's still loyal to my da."

"If the Advocate *could* get here before the guards, there might not need to be any fighting at all," Quellin said. "Which is what we've been aiming for."

"Yes, but we can't count on that," Elson said. "We have to assume that the guards will arrive first, and plan tactics to stall them until the Advocate gets here. How can we get a message back to Salima without a pigeon?"

"There's a ferry rower named Penyard. I've known him all my life," Callian said. "We can trust him. And Senior Salima introduced me to a girl who's helping her—"

"Trixin!" Raffa and Kuma said together.

"Yes, that's right," Callian said.

"Good, then," Haddie said. "We'll get a message to

Mannum Penyard, for Trixin to take to Salima." She turned and began walking back into the clearing, with most of the council following her.

"I'll put up your horse for you," Fitzer said. "Raffa, Kuma, maybe you could see that our guest gets to eat and rest."

"Thank you," Callian said politely. Before he handed over the reins, he spoke briefly to the horse. "Mal, this man is going to take care of you," he said. "Go with him, okay?" The horse touched Callian's arm with its nose and nickered.

Callian gave Fitzer the reins, then said, "There's one more thing." He opened the nearest of the two saddlebags.

Raffa was standing close enough to see an animal's head emerge from the bag. At first he thought it was a cat, but then he saw the distinctive black-and-white mask around its eyes.

A raccoon . . . ?

Callian held out his arm, and the raccoon trundled right up to his shoulder, where it perched, looking around curiously and sniffing the air. It sniffed in Raffa's direction, once, twice—and then let out a shrill squeak.

"Twig?" the raccoon said.

Raffa froze, his mouth a perfect circle of surprise. He stared and blinked and stared again, and finally managed to speak.

"*Bando?* Is that you?"

"Twig? Twig? Twig! Twig!"

CHAPTER THIRTEEN

K UMA was already off, darting between the tents and then into the Forest, to search for Twig, Bando's twin sister. Raffa led Callian, holding Bando, to the pother tent. Garith and Jimble were not there; Raffa guessed that they were out gathering nettles.

Once inside, Callian put the raccoon down on the floor.

"Twig? Twig?" Bando said, looking at Raffa.

Raffa smiled. "I think it's my scent," he said to Callian. "He remembers that the last time he was with me Twig was there. She's his sister."

Then he paused for a moment, needing to ask a question but half-dreading the answer. "My mam," he said. "When you last saw her, was she . . . all right?"

Callian nodded. "She said I was to tell you not to worry about her. And that she's being allowed to visit your da."

Raffa stood motionless, as if not moving would help him contain the feelings that flooded through him: Relief on hearing that his mother was fine coupled with an ache at missing both his parents that felt sharp enough to cut his insides.

Callian waited in silence for a moment, then changed the subject. "I found him months ago," he said, looking at Bando fondly. The raccoon had discovered a basket and was digging through it. "Last fall."

That made sense. Raffa had left Gilden in the fall, along with Garith and Kuma, accompanied by Echo, Roo, and Twig. Bando and the mother raccoon had been with them at first, but had gotten lost along the way.

"Was his mother with him? Or did you see her nearby?"

Callian shook his head. "He was alone and scared. Crying. I wouldn't have taken him if he'd been with his mother."

Then he gave Raffa a look. "You're not asking the right question."

Raffa stiffened a little. "What do you mean by that?"

Callian was studying him intently. "You don't seem the least bit surprised that he was saying 'Twig.' He can say 'Mama,' too, and a few other words, but I have a feeling you already knew that."

"Oh." Raffa blushed. "Um. Well, it's an awfully long story. . . ."

"And a good one, I'm sure upon certain. You don't have to tell me now, but I hope to hear it someday." He spread his hands in a gesture of good-natured patience.

Raffa relaxed a little, and squatted down on the floor to watch Bando. The curious raccoon was pulling items out of the basket one by one: a strainer, tongs, some clay jars.

"He can say 'eat,' and some food words," Callian said. "Grubs—he loves grubs."

Bando's head swiveled toward Callian, eyes bright with interest. "Grub?" Bando asked. "Grub?"

Raffa smiled. "Twig loves grubs, too."

"Sorry," Callian said to Bando, "no grubs now. But we can try to find some later." Bando chirruped and went back to examining a jar.

Kuma burst into the tent, Twig on her shoulders. Panting, she reached up to disengage Twig's paws from her hair.

"I had a bit of a time," she said. "She didn't want to leave Roo."

"Roo?" Callian asked.

"Er, part of that same story," Raffa answered. Kuma's friendship with the giant golden bear wasn't easy to explain quickly.

Fortunately, a welcome distraction was at hand. Kuma put Twig on the ground. Bando was on the other side of the tent; he had not yet noticed his twin sister's arrival.

Twig sniffed the air, looking around. Her head stopped moving abruptly as soon as she caught Bando's scent.

"Bando? Bando?" she squeaked, and trundled across the floor in his direction.

Then she stopped short and cocked her head. "Bando?"

All three humans shouted with laughter, for Twig was staring in puzzlement at a furry creature whose head was a clay jar.

* * *

After Callian extracted Bando's head from the jar, the twins' reunion was a joyful flurry of squeaks and chirps, pawing and wrestling, nuzzles and cooing. But it ended almost as quickly as it began. Bando went back to the basket, and Twig started a tour of the whole tent.

"I guess she's more attached to Roo now than she is to him," Kuma observed.

Callian nodded. "And he— Well, I guess we kind of adopted each other," he said. "We've been together every day since I found him."

Raffa saw that the eyes of both raccoons still had the same faint purple sheen as Echo's. All three animals had been treated with the scarlet vine, which had turned their eyes purple. The violet hue had faded with time, but could still be seen in the right light.

"Was he ever sick?" The question came to Raffa abruptly, surprising even him. "Bando, I mean."

"Sick? Not really," Callian answered. "Once he had some tummy trouble—he found a stash of dried plums and ate too many. Otherwise, he's been really healthy."

Raffa looked at Kuma, who nodded; she knew what he was thinking. Animals treated with the scarlet vine eventually suffered from life-threatening side effects. But the raccoons seem to have been spared this fate because they had been dosed with the vine infusion only once, not repeatedly.

Raffa felt himself teetering on the brink of an important revelation. Wordless, indistinct, the thought might well vanish into nothingness. He held his breath, unsure whether to focus or to let his mind drift.

Echo and Bando and Twig. The scarlet vine. Purple eyes . . .

Realization struck him then—so hard that he caught his breath and choked, coughing several times.

"Raffa?" Kuma turned toward him in concern.

"The animals . . . ," he croaked. He swallowed hard and cleared his throat. "They must all be addicted now, right? Like the fox at the settlement? So they're being dosed, again and again, to keep them under control until—until they've done what they've been trained to do."

He didn't have to say it; she and Callian both understood. *Until they've attacked as many Afters as they can, and driven the rest away.*

"Then what?" Raffa continued. "The dosing has to stop sometime—there isn't enough of the scarlet vine. Without being dosed, the animals will all be twitchy and—and unpredictable, like that fox at the settlement. And that will make them dangerous."

He put his hands to his head and tugged on his hair in agitation. "So the Chancellor could order that they all be killed. And even if they aren't . . . if they're released, they'll be so sick, most of them probably won't make it."

Kuma was staring at him in horror. "Are you saying that . . . they're all doomed?"

Raffa took a breath to steady himself and his voice. "No. But their only chance is for us to succeed. To delay the attack, to stall the guards as long as we can, so the Advocate can get here."

He raised his hands in a half-shrug. "We're trying to save people, and if we do, we might be able to save the animals, too."

He left unsaid the other possibility: That failure would be disastrous for both.

"I understand what you're saying," Callian said slowly. "But the timing matters, too, doesn't it? If the guards get here before my da does, they'll send the animals to attack. We'll have no choice but to kill or at least injure as many as we can—even if we eventually end up winning."

"You can save them, can't you?" Kuma said, her voice pitched high in anxiety. "With the antidote? Remember the fox? He ran off—he didn't want anything to do with humans. If we could get all those animals to do the same—"

"How?" Raffa snapped, cutting her off. "How can we dose them in the middle of a *battle*, for quake's sake?"

"You're the pother. *You* figure it out," she snapped right back at him.

Raffa knew that he wasn't really upset with Kuma, but it felt like she was putting too much pressure on him, to solve a problem that had no solution. They glared at each other for a long moment. He could hear his own angry breathing.

Then Callian said, "This is where I clear my throat to break the awkward silence."

He cleared his throat, exaggerating the sound for several counts. Raffa and Kuma both blinked—and laughed.

Callian grinned. "Whew. It worked."

Raffa looked at Kuma. "Dosing them with the antidote—that's the answer. I have no idea *how*, but I do know one thing: We can't do it without the cavern plant. . . . So I have to go back to the gorge."

CHAPTER FOURTEEN

RAFFA went first to the council. He explained the
need to travel to the gorge to collect the cavern
plant. Not only did he receive permission, but Fitzer volunteered to drive him.

"Where is it you're headed?" Fitzer asked.

"Just beyond the Southern Woodlands," Raffa replied.

"If I can borrow a second horse for the wagon, we
should be able to get there by late afternoon," Fitzer said,
"and there'll be a moon, so we can travel back tonight.
Are you ready?"

"Almost." They agreed to meet in the area where

the wagons and horses were being kept—a stable constructed of canvas and poles at the edge of the clearing near the path.

Raffa stopped at the pantry tent to fetch some food, both for his trip to the gorge and for Callian. When he returned to the pother tent, Jimble and Garith were back from their nettle-gathering expedition. Garith was already applying a poultice to Jimble's hands, where he'd obviously been stung several times by nettles.

"Weren't you wearing gloves?" Raffa asked.

"I was!" Jimble said. "But I took them off—just once." He mimed taking off gloves, then held up his index finger. "I never been stung by a nettle before. I figured I should know what it feels like."

Raffa had to smile. *He's so eager. He's like a puppy bouncing around—a really smart one. That has thumbs.*

"Garith, will you make the combination for the antidote?" Raffa asked. "Mellia, ranagua berries, panax root."

"Stimulant proportions?" Garith asked.

Raffa nodded. "Powder, not liquid." He made sprinkling motions with his fingers. Although he still didn't know how he would dose the animals, it would be easier to transport in powdered form and could always be turned back into a liquid if necessary. "I hope you won't have trouble finding the panax."

"I can help with that," Kuma said. "I know where it's likely to be growing."

Raffa went to meet Mannum Fitzer. He walked through the tent camp, which buzzed with activity. Some people were still setting up tents; others were carrying boxes and bundles. No one was idle; even the small children were busy, collecting twigs for kindling. Clearly, it took a great deal of work to shelter people who had lost their homes.

They followed the path out of the clearing, then the road to the south. Raffa and Fitzer took it in turns to drive so the other person could sleep, both of them having been up all night during the river crossing. When they reached the foothills, they shared a snack of crackerbread with cheese and dried tomatoes.

It was chilly but sunny, a day more spring than winter. With the wagon bed empty, the horses kept up a good pace with ease. Raffa wished he could enjoy the ride, but they had to keep a constant eye out for guards. At the first settlement they came to, Fitzer spoke to a man he knew, who reported that guards had been through earlier but had already returned to Gilden. After that, Raffa relaxed a little—only to find that his mind filled up right away with worry.

He was desperate for a moment of intuition—one that would help him figure out how to treat the animals. But he knew such moments came when he least expected them.

The gorge was as Raffa remembered it. Steep cliffs rose on either side of the river, which was only two paces wide here. Small trees and hardy shrubs grew from cracks in the rock face. Fitzer watered the horses, then tied them to an oak at the base of the northern cliff.

Searching carefully, Raffa located a partially uprooted neverbare tree leaning against the rock face. It had been pulled up by Roo, at Kuma's request, to serve as a marker. He began to climb, taking the lead to show Fitzer the way.

When Raffa reached the right ledge, he pulled himself over the edge and sat for a moment of rest. Echo emerged from under his tunic, clicking and chirping in excitement.

"Echo friend many!" he squeaked.

Afternoon was edging into evening, but it was still a little earlier than Echo's usual waking time. Clearly, the bat had sensed where they were: The gorge was riddled with caves that were home to thousands of bats, and Echo had socialized with some of them during the previous visit to the cavern.

"We're not going to be here long, Echo," Raffa cautioned him. "We'll be leaving soon. Come find me a few times, and I'll whistle when it's time to leave."

Echo fluttered to the entrance of the cave at the back of the ledge. "Friend many!" he squeaked again before disappearing into the cave.

This time, the collection of the cavern plant would be much easier, with Fitzer there to help. In addition to his own leather rope, Raffa had come equipped with another rope of hemp and several sacks.

Raffa led the way down the narrow passageway to the cavern. He stopped at the big boulder to tie the hemp rope in place, then continued to where the passage appeared to end in a solid wall of rock. But there was a crevice in the wall just wide enough for him to slip through.

Here they ran into their first hitch: Fitzer could not squeeze through the crevice. He tried several times and would have kept trying, but Raffa made him stop.

"What if you get stuck and I can't get you out? I've

done this before on my own. I'll be fine."

They agreed that Raffa would tie *both* ropes around himself, just in case one failed, and that Fitzer would haul him up when he was ready. Once through the crevice, Raffa shinned carefully over the edge of the huge rock there, and landed on the narrow ledge that rimmed the cavern.

He paused for a moment to look around the vast space. The strange and beautiful cavern plants lit up at intervals, whenever hot gases from deep within the earth bubbled up in the cavern's lake. He shivered at the memory of his last visit, when he had fallen into the water, with no way to get out. Echo had saved him by dropping Raffa's trusty leather rope over a high crag, then rounding up hundreds of bats to pin the rope in place.

"All steady in there?" Fitzer called through the crevice.

"Steady," Raffa replied, and got to work.

He was pleased to see that the plants were recovering since he had harvested from among them a few weeks earlier; there was already new growth. He stripped off all his clothes and went into the water naked. Paddling around the edge of the cavern, he collected three of every four plants. It was more than he normally would have taken, given that the plant was so unusual. But the need was desperate. He was careful to leave the roots of each plant intact, which he hoped would ensure their recovery.

In a short time, he had filled six large bags. The plants that remained cast a much dimmer glow; the cavern now seemed a far gloomier place. He was relieved to call out to Fitzer.

"I'm finished. You can pull me up now."

Back in his dry clothes, Raffa roped two of the bags of plants to his back; Fitzer took the other four. They climbed back down the cliff and loaded the wagon, working quickly.

The last of the sun's rays carved deep shadows in the gorge. Fitzer untied the horses. Raffa climbed onto the wagon seat and glanced up for a last look at the ledge that marked the entrance to the cavern.

"Look!" He pointed overhead.

A colony of bats was emerging from a crack in the cliff face. Raffa and Fitzer watched, their faces turned skyward, as more bats took wing.

Raffa had witnessed this exodus on his last visit to the cavern, but that time he had been inside the passageway.

Bats had flown past him in what had seemed like a never-ending stream, but he now realized that he had seen only a fraction of the number that lived inside the cliff.

What he and Fitzer were seeing was truly spectacular. Not hundreds but *thousands* of bats poured out of the cliff's caves and crevices, their beautiful wings beating and flickering, sometimes shining when the sun's rays hit them. The bats filled the sky as if an enormous lacy blanket had been thrown over the gorge, a blanket that was constantly moving and yet always overhead.

Every time Raffa thought they must surely have seen the last of them, another great skein of bats would appear. He did not know how long they had been watching, but when the bats finally vanished from view, he and Fitzer continued to sit in silence, spelled by wonder.

Fitzer spoke first. "Well," he said, "that was special."

Raffa cleared his throat. "I guess we should get on," he said. "I just have to call my bat."

He stood up and gave a sharp whistle. "Echo!" he called. "Echo, time to go!"

His voice carried well in the narrow gorge, but after the sound died away, the air around him was silent.

He tried again, whistling twice this time. "ECHO! Where are you?"

Still no response. Raffa tutted in annoyance. "Sorry," he said to Fitzer. "He's usually good about coming when I whistle. I guess I'll have to go back up again."

He was tired now, and the climb to the ledge seemed twice as high as it had the first time. Once, his foot slipped, and he grabbed at a jutting crag just in time, banging his chin. "Quake's sake, Echo, why can't you come when I whistle?" he muttered angrily.

At the back of the ledge was the opening that led to the cavern, as well as the countless cracks and crevices where the bats lived. Raffa slipped inside and walked a few steps down the narrow passage.

"Echo!" he shouted. "ECHO!"

—*echo—echo—echo*—

Any other time, he might have smiled at the irony—Echo's name echoing—but it occurred to him then that the bat hadn't checked in with him since their arrival at the gorge. That had never happened before. Was something wrong? Could Echo have gotten injured somehow?

Not likely. The cliff was a safe place for the bats; it was why they roosted there. Raffa listened hard for any sound, but heard nothing. The silence felt almost solid.

His knees began to tremble. He pushed away his next

thought, but it came back, pummeling and battering at his brain. . . .

Echo was there. *With all the others.*

Echo had been somewhere in the midst of that incredible massive cloud of bats.

Raffa backed out of the passage and looked up. The sky was blank now, not a single bat to be seen. It was as if they had never been there at all.

"Friend many". . . *He was so excited about seeing them again. I should have known, I could have—*

Could have what? Tied Echo to the perch to keep him from seeing his friends?

No. I'd never— I want him to be happy. Of course I do.

He closed his eyes and leaned his forehead against the stone face of the cliff, knowing in his heart that it would be useless to whistle or call again. Echo had finally left him—had gone back to the wild to live with other bats for good.

"Raffa?" Fitzer called from below.

Raffa stayed still for another moment. "Coming," he mumbled, then straightened up slowly and walked to the rim of the ledge.

"Coming," he said again, and waved at Fitzer.

In a daze of disbelief, he half-climbed and half-slid down the cliff, collecting bruises and scratches that he didn't feel. All the while, his gut twisted slowly. *Pain* was not the right word; it was too far inside him. Pain was something that happened to your skin or your bones or other parts of your body. This was deeper than that. He didn't want to cry. He wanted to curl up in a ball and never move again.

At the base of the cliff, he stared into the sky one last time.

I never even got to say good-bye.

Somehow that seemed monstrously unfair.

It took the last of his strength to pull himself up onto the wagon seat. "Let's go," he said to Fitzer, through wooden lips.

Fitzer looked at him for a long breath, then nodded and flicked the reins.

PART II

CHAPTER FIFTEEN

RAFFA took over the driving; he needed something to do. When they reached camp, he unloaded the wagon while Fitzer took care of the horses. A three-quarter moon rose as Raffa trundled a fully loaded wheelbarrow through the camp. He left it just outside the pother tent; there was something he needed to do before he began his work with the cavern plant.

Most of the camp's denizens were at the central pavilion for the evening meal, which suited him perfectly. He didn't want to run into anyone. Head down, he shuffled toward Elson and Haddie's tent. Kuma probably wouldn't be there, but he had decided to try the tent first, rather than face the crowds in the pavilion.

"Kuma?" he called.

He was in luck. The tent flap opened. Kuma stepped out, took one look at his face, and said, "What's wrong?"

He shrugged and stubbed the toe of his boot in the dirt. "Echo . . ." He could not go on.

"Is he"—she took a breath—"is he okay?"

He looked up and blinked. Such a simple question, and yet the most important one she could have asked.

"Yes. Yes, he's okay. He—he didn't come back with me. He stayed in the gorge. With the other bats."

"Oh." A pause, and she put a hand on his arm. "He's safer there, don't you think? Away from people. Especially because of that coin reward."

She was right, but he wasn't ready to admit it. He shrugged again, his head down.

Her eyes were wide with sympathy, but her voice was firm. "Do you remember what I told you, about when I first met Roo? And then we got separated, and I didn't know where she was, and it took us years to find each other again? You're lucky—you know exactly where Echo is. You'll see him again. I'm sure of it."

Raffa nodded. He'd gotten what he came for. He hadn't known what Kuma would say, but he knew he would feel better after talking to her.

And he did. Not a lot better but a little better, and that would have to do for now.

"There was some news while you were gone," Kuma said. She explained that a runner had arrived late in the afternoon. "The guard troops are gathering along the river on the Gilden side, and they're setting up camp. But it's not going well for them. A whole bunch of guards have deserted, saying that they won't fight in the Forest, that they're afraid of strange beasts and giant bears and things like that. So they're having to regroup and reorganize. We're fairly certain nothing will happen tonight or tomorrow."

Tonight. Tomorrow. "I better get that antidote made," he mumbled.

"I'll be along later to help," she said.

As Raffa walked back to the pother tent, he knew how he could take his mind off of Echo: by keeping himself occupied. That will be easy, he thought with grim determination. He would start by converting the cavern plant into a powder.

At the pother tent he saw that Garith and Jimble had been very busy during his absence. Both boys had patches of red rash on their cheeks, and one of Jimble's eyes was almost swollen shut. Raffa recognized the usual consequences of working with nettles; even the most careful apothecaries often ended up with a rash.

In addition to the bucket full of nettle essence, which Raffa recognized by its sharp green smell, there were two basins on the table. Raffa stepped closer and sniffed at the first basin. It was the stimulant combination.

"You found panax?" he asked.

"Kuma did," Garith replied. "Never thought I'd meet someone who knows the Forest better than a pother." He nodded in admiration.

"I'm going to start boiling down the cavern plant next," Raffa said as he examined the paste in the second basin. It definitely included romarian, another easily recognizable odor. The smell was vaguely familiar, but he couldn't quite place it. "What's this?"

Garith gave him a sly grin. "C, R, D," he answered.

"What?"

Garith said nothing more. He stood there with an incredibly annoying smirk on his face, as if saying, *Come now, little cousin, you can do it, you can figure this out if you really try. . . .*

C, R, D? A fine chord of memory twanged in Raffa's mind, its vibrations growing stronger until finally the right part of his brain was shaken awake.

C, R, D! The mysterious letters on the jar in the cupboard hidden under the stairs . . . the jar that held the combination he and Garith had experimented with months ago—before Echo, before Gilden, before the Chancellor. A lifetime ago.

The unknown combination, made into a poultice, had given both boys glowing blue veins in their cheeks. Later, they had learned that the mystery ingredients were candleplant, romarian, and duckberry.

"Oh!" Raffa exclaimed. "But why—what—"

Garith shrugged as the smirk slid off his face. "I'm not sure," he admitted. "I just thought that if the guards attack at night, we should have a way to mark ourselves that would show up in the dark. I don't know . . . I thought it might be useful. Putting this on our faces would be better than having to carry lightsticks—it would leave our hands free. And when we don't need the glow, we can pull down those masks to cover it."

"That's amazing!" Raffa enthused. "It's a great idea. I'm sure we can find a way to use it."

Then he stopped short, recalling the poultice episode: Garith's batch, unlike his own, had resulted in dreadful swelling.

"I know what you're thinking," Garith said loudly. "I'll tell you exactly what happened. It got all bubbly, but it was too stiff. So I added both oil and water, and it came out really smooth, just like yours was last time." A pause. "You think I didn't notice the difference? I did. I always do." He shrugged. "I used to hope it wouldn't matter."

Used to . . . , Raffa thought.

Something had shifted in his relationship with Garith. They had been born cousins and had become friends. But when it came to apothecary, they had always been rivals.

Now, instead of rivals, they were partners, and Raffa was surprised by the relief and satisfaction he felt on realizing this. But of course he wasn't going to say anything about it; he wasn't sure he could have put it into words.

"We should tell the council," he said, "so they can figure out how to work it into the battle plans."

"Not just yet," Garith said. "I wasn't sure about the proportions. I tried to go by what I remembered about the smell. It still has to be tested."

"I'll do it!" Jimble volunteered eagerly.

Raffa rolled his eyes. In Gilden, Jimble had played

a heroic role in a scheme by drinking a botanical combination—and throwing up a rainbow. Now he seemed to think that testing botanicals and combinations was his special purview.

"On your hand," Garith said.

Jimble stuck his finger in the poultice and rubbed it vigorously onto the back of his hand. All three of them stared at the spot, unblinking.

Nothing happened for several moments. But then a faint glimmer appeared, and quickly became a strong and steady blue glow—with no swelling.

"Look! Look!" Jimble shouted. He raised both hands overhead, even though only one of them was glowing blue, and spoke in a gravelly roar. "I AM THE BLUE-HANDED BEASTER. KNEEL BEFORE ME OR DIE!"

"Oh, for quake's sake," Raffa said, but he couldn't help laughing.

"At least we know it works," Garith said.

Boiling down the cavern plant would require an all-night vigil at the fire pit. Raffa wanted to write a list of tasks on the tabletop, just as his father had always done, but he couldn't find any chalk. He made a list in his head instead.

Rinse plants well. Check for insects.

Strip leaves.

Chop stems.

At fire pit: Boil stems to extract essence. Add leaves near the end. Strain.

Boil essence down to residue.

Raffa emptied a bag of plants onto the tabletop. He examined the first plant, then tossed it into a basin of water.

On the second plant, he found a small beetle. He shook it off the plant and into his palm.

"What is it?" Jimble asked.

"Just a beetle," Raffa answered.

It was the same kind of beetle that Echo had eaten when he was sick. He'd gotten better very quickly, and had been well ever since. The beetles had been feeding on the cavern plant, which was what had given Raffa the idea that the plant might be an antidote for the ailments caused by the scarlet-vine infusion.

If it hadn't been for Echo, he never would have found the cavern or the plant.

How long will it be before I see him again? Be safe, Echo. Be careful—watch out for owls. . . .

He closed his hand gently around the insect, took it to the tent flap, and released it outside.

His thoughts had led him to a new conclusion. *Making the antidote and treating all those animals with it— I mean, if I can figure out how, it will be sort of like finishing the work that Echo helped me start. A way to—to keep him with me, even though he's not here.*

He lifted his chin as he went back to the worktable. This was much better: Not staying busy to take his mind off Echo, but working hard precisely because Echo was on his mind.

CHAPTER SIXTEEN

SOON the cleaned cavern plants were simmering in two gigantic cauldrons. Raffa had never before made such an enormous batch of solution. The cauldrons were too big and heavy to empty by upending them. To strain the solution, he and the others began the long, clumsy process of ladling the hot liquid through a sieve into jars.

"Yow!" Jimble screeched. He had splashed some of the essence on himself. "I'm okay, I'm fine, no worries," he added hastily.

Then Kuma went off and returned with two baskets, which they could lower into the cauldrons to scoop out the solids. It was still slow work, but easier than ladling.

Finally all the plant matter had been removed. Next, the liquid essence would be boiled down to a dry residue, which required careful watching, especially at the end of the process. If it boiled too long, the residue would burn; not long enough, it would remain dissolved in the water.

At the beginning of the boil-down, when the cauldrons were both three-quarters full, Raffa did not have to keep his eyes on them every second. Jimble had dozed off, leaning against a stump. Raffa woke him and sent him to bed. The last thing Raffa needed was a sleepy assistant, what with the fire and the large quantities of scalding liquid. He knew that Jimble was exhausted, because the boy went to the tents without a word of protest.

Raffa took a lightstick and held it up to his face. With Kuma at his side, he nudged Garith and stood facing him squarely.

"I still haven't figured out how to dose the animals," he said. The words rasped as they came out, his throat thick with anxiety.

This was everything. The problem had never been far from the front of his mind, no matter what else he was thinking.

The guards would send the animals to attack first. That was a guess, but one that the council had agreed made sense: Why risk injury to people when you could use animals instead? Only after the animals attacked would the guards engage in the fighting themselves.

If Raffa couldn't figure out a way to treat the animals with the antidote, the Afters would have no choice but to defend themselves, meaning that both humans and beasts would get hurt.

Or worse.

Raffa had worn out his brain trying to think of a way to get the antidote into the animals' food source. It was how he had treated a few dozen animals before. But he could not use the same strategy again: Trixin had told him that the compound now had a much heavier guard presence. And even if he could manage it somehow, he would also have to make sure that the animals weren't dosed again with the vine infusion, which would undo the effects of the antidote.

His thoughts had gone in circles so many times that he was actually starting to feel nauseated.

"I've been thinking about that, too," Garith replied. "Inhalation, right?"

Raffa stared at him. Of course! The quickest way to

get a substance into the bloodstream was by inhaling it. "Like the dogs and the throx!" he exclaimed. Why hadn't he thought of it before?

But Garith was shaking his head. "It wouldn't work the same way," he said. "Those dogs—their *job* is to sniff, that's what they've been trained to do. The attack animals, if we scatter the antidote powder on the ground, I'm guessing most of them *won't* stop to sniff at it, not if they've been well trained."

"That's it, isn't it?" Raffa said slowly. "Predictability. We *knew* what the dogs would do."

His heart thumped harder. He had a feeling that their discussion held the key to the answer.

Predictability. So what do we know about the animals? What can we count on them to do for sure?

He thought again about the animals at the riverbank, and the attack on Kuma's settlement. And the fox he and Kuma had healed.

Red, spring . . . Red, spring . . .

Kuma met his gaze. "They jump," she said.

He nodded. "They've been trained to leap at people's throats," he said. "Not the badgers—they go for people's ankles, to trip them up. But the foxes and stoats, they attack by jumping." He gestured with his hands as

Garith watched him intently.

"Sooo . . . ," Garith said, "how can we use that?"

On impulse, Raffa decided to try something he'd never done before. He closed his eyes and rolled his shoulders to relax them. Then he let images float freely in his mind's eye. The fox jumping. Stoats snapping. The cavern plant glowing, the cauldrons boiling, the fine-grained antidote powder.

He was trying to *summon* a moment of intuition. *It probably won't work. They have to just come to me on their own. I can't force them. . . .*

True enough, he saw or felt nothing unusual. *Don't give up. Try, just a little longer.*

The fox jumping. It jumped higher and higher. On its last jump, it landed—with a bottle in its mouth. The bottle disappeared. The fox seemed to be smiling. It licked its lips, then vanished with a jaunty wave of its brushy tail.

A bottle?

In a far corner of Raffa's mind, he was exultant: He had done it! *And it wasn't even that hard.* He wondered if it was because of the time he had already spent thinking about the problem. *It's like . . . that part of my brain was ready. All the frustration—it was practice, or exercise—*

"Raffa? Raffa, are you okay?"

The voice seemed very faint; he could hardly hear it. Then Kuma waved a hand in front of his face.

He shook his head as if he were shaking off sleep. When his vision cleared, he saw Garith and Kuma both staring at him.

"Listen," he said, "I know this is going to sound crazy, but I need your help."

Another first: He had never discussed his intuitions with anyone else before. They were too hard to explain. Like the tunnel and the touchrue thorns: That feeling of moving through the tunnel and bursting out of the end was an analogy for thorns shooting through a reed. He had figured that one out quickly enough, but other intuitions had taken him hours or even days to decipher.

They didn't have that kind of time.

"In my head I saw a fox jumping," he began, "and when he landed, he had a bottle in his mouth. What do you think that means?"

Garith frowned. Kuma gaped. They both looked completely bewildered.

"Okay, forget that. Just think about a bottle. When I say 'bottle,' what comes into your head? Fast—don't think, just say words."

This was often how his intuitions worked—seemingly at random, their logic buried deep. "Just trust me," he said. "Please?"

"Okay," Garith said, "bottle. Um—they're made of clay?"

"Or glass," Kuma said, "the fancy ones."

"Round," Garith said. "Er, I mean, cylinder."

"Cork."

"Cork, stopper."

"Good," Raffa encouraged. "Keep going."

"What are we trying to do?" Garith asked.

"I don't know," Raffa admitted. "But I think I'll know when we get there."

"Breakable," Kuma said.

"Um . . . liquid. They hold liquid?" Garith was clearly growing impatient.

"Liquid. Pour. Spill." Kuma was still trying.

"Neck," Garith said. "Bottles have necks— Faults and fissures! What are we *doing* here?"

Raffa didn't answer; in fact, he hadn't heard anything Garith had said after the word *neck*. A bottle's neck . . . It was there, somewhere. Again, his mind sank into itself; for how long, he didn't know.

"—can't think of anything else," Kuma was saying.

Raffa bounced up and down on his toes. "You did it," he said, trying to keep his voice calm. "I figured it out—an idea that I think will work." He looked from Kuma's face to Garith's. "But we're going to need everybody's help. Everybody."

CHAPTER SEVENTEEN

A T daybirth the next morning, the sun rose on the clearing, which was quiet and still. No one was bustling amidst the tents as they had been the day before. Instead, the settlers and escaped Gildeners were sitting in small clusters throughout the camp. Only their hands were busy, engaged in one of three activities: whittling, knitting, or unraveling.

The whittlers had piles of sticks beside them. They stripped the bark from each stick, smoothed the wood underneath, and sharpened one end. They were making knitting needles.

As soon as they finished a pair, one of the knitters

would snatch it up and begin knitting furiously, using yarn provided by the unravelers. Every available knitted garment in the camp—scarves, sweaters, shawls, caps—was being unraveled, a task easy enough for the younger children.

Raffa had made samples from an unraveled scarf. He had knitted long narrow sacks in two sizes, one the length of his foot, the other twice that. Each was as big around as an ax handle. He sewed one end shut but left the other open, with a length of yarn hanging free. Now he moved from group to group, showing the knitters the samples, so they would know what to make.

"You need to make them for every adult and teen in your family," he said. "Everyone will need at least two of each size, and more would be better." He repeated this over and over; Kuma helped him spread the word.

"When we're done here, the council wants to see us," she said.

The first of the sacks were completed by the fastest knitters. Children around eight or nine years of age served as runners, collecting the sacks and delivering them to the apothecary tent, where Jimble and Garith were working together. After making his way around the whole camp, Raffa went to see how they were doing.

Two huge bags of powder sat on the worktable. Garith held a funnel; Jimble, a small scoop, which he waved at Raffa.

"I'm not wasting a single bit," Jimble said earnestly. "Watch!"

The cavern-plant residue was now a powder; it had been scraped and pulverized in the darkest hours before daybirth. Raffa had added the powder to the panax combination Garith had made. He took a little linen bag, filled it with two scoops of the powder, and put it away in his rucksack for a special task he wanted to work on later.

Garith stretched the open end of a knitted sack around the tip of the funnel and held it in place. Jimble took a scoopful of the powder combination and carefully poured it into the funnel's mouth. He was frowning in concentration, his tongue stuck out. Over his head, Garith caught Raffa's eye and winked, obviously amused and impressed by Jimble's interest in apothecary.

When the little sack was filled with powder, Garith tied off the opening with the loose end of yarn. Then he took short pieces of yarn and tied them tightly around the sack in two places. The sack now looked like three linked sausages. A pile of them was growing in a basket on the floor.

"See?" Jimble said. "We could go faster, but I think it's more important not to spill the powder. That's right, isn't it?"

Raffa agreed. Jimble glowed.

Satisfied with their progress, Raffa went to the council meeting.

Raffa saw Kuma sitting next to Elson, and took a seat between her and Quellin, with Haddie opposite him.

"What's this about?" he whispered. He had spoken to the council in the hour before dawn, a long discussion during which he explained the strategy for the antidote. He and Kuma and Garith had been up all night, tending the cavern-plant solution and talking over the strategy from every possible angle.

"Not sure," she whispered back, "but at least they're knitting." Each council member was busy with a pair of homemade needles in their hands.

"Good," Haddie said. "This will be quick, we all have a lot of work to do."

Elson turned to look at Raffa and Kuma. "You know

that our overall objective is delay," he said. "We've got the blowpipes, and these—" He held up the half-finished sack on his knitting needles. "But that's not enough."

He put down his knitting and placed a hand on Kuma's shoulder. "Kuma, we'd like you to consider something."

She barely let him finish. "No," she said, crossing her arms in a stubborn gesture and leaning slightly away from him. "*No*."

How did she know what he was going to say? Raffa wondered. But in the next moment, he knew, too.

There was only one possible strategy that Kuma alone would be able to implement—and she had just said no.

She would never agree to using Roo in battle.

Haddie looked resigned. "We expected that," she said. "Kuma, please talk it over with Raffa. No one wants to hurt the bear, but if she can help us . . ." Her voice trailed off.

Kuma shook her head and said it again.

"No."

Raffa left the circle with Kuma, and together they walked toward the pother tent. "We need to collect touchrue thorns," he said. "Will you come with me?"

"I know where there's a heavy stand of them," she said, "and it's not far from where Roo and Twig are, so we can check on them, too."

They fetched buckets, gloves, and snippers from the pother tent, and set off. Kuma led the way east out of the clearing.

"Roo is so happy to be back in the Forest," she said. "She's showing Twig everything. They're having a grand time."

"That's good," Raffa said. The two animals were a little family, and they were home again.

He thought of his own home and family—Da in his cell at the Garrison, Mam creeping around the Commons trying to free the Advocate, their cabin burned to ashes. . . . When would they ever be together again?

Then he experienced a moment of terrible clarity. *Home.* The captive animals had been taken from their homes and the Afters were being chased from theirs, acts of cruelty and callousness that had to be defied.

He spoke at once. "You're right, Kuma," he said, "about what the Chancellor is doing—how wrong it all is. And if she wins, who knows what else she'll do? We *have* to stop her. We have to use every single thing we have. You can see that, can't you?"

She looked startled at the abrupt change of subject, but he had to finish what he was saying. He glared at her. Part of him hated what he was doing; another part of him knew that it had to be done.

"You know what it means, Kuma: *Roo. We need Roo.*"

Kuma shook her head, crossed her arms, and turned one shoulder away from him. But Raffa saw the expression on her face: She was thinking hard rather than instantly saying no.

He gave her a moment to herself. When he spoke, he made sure that his voice was gentle.

"Kuma . . . What if we could think of a way to—to have Roo help us without putting her in danger?" Quickly he amended his words. "Or, I mean, as little danger as possible."

She tilted her head to let him know that she was listening.

"Er, I actually don't have any idea how we would do that," he admitted. "Maybe together we could think of something?"

When she didn't reply, he shrugged. *I mustn't push her too hard.* "So where are those touchrues?"

The shrubs were scattered among tangles of bramble

and shagneedle bushes. The growth in the Forest was budding out; twigs and branches were mostly bare. The puffy shagneedles kept their dried foliage through the winter and were just starting to shed; Raffa thought they looked like enormous untidy hedgehogs.

Raffa and Kuma donned gloves and took up their snippers. They began clipping the large vicious-looking thorns one by one into the buckets.

It took a long time to fill all four buckets. Raffa's hands ached from the repeated motion of snipping. And even with gloves on, both he and Kuma suffered from inevitable scratches. He had brought along a soothing poultice; between them they used every last smear of it.

Kuma had spent some time with Callian, the Advocate's son, while Raffa had been away at the gorge. "What's he like?" Raffa asked.

To his surprise, Kuma ducked her head in an attempt to hide a shy smile, and Raffa could have sworn she was blushing.

She shrugged. "He's okay, I guess," she said, her voice nonchalant.

But she couldn't hold back her interest. "Did you know that he's half-Hangullite?" Hangull was a land to the west, far beyond Obsidia's borders.

"He's an After?" Raffa was startled.

"No, not exactly. His mom's family, they came to Obsidia from Hangull *before* the Quake. They were diplomats, or something—a group of them traveled here to make an alliance. The Quake happened while they were here, so they never left. Their whole country was destroyed, and then some other Hangullites came here, so those ones *are* Afters."

Most Hangullites had high cheekbones. Raffa hadn't noticed before, but now he recalled Callian's features, and it made sense that he had Hangullite blood.

"Anyway, he seems steady," Kuma said. "I like the way he treats Bando. More like a—a friend than a pet."

Raffa felt an empty chill at his neckline, in the space where Echo used to hang on the perch necklace. He wondered if he would ever get used to missing the little bat.

With a sigh, Raffa peered into his second bucket, which was nearly full. One more shrub, he thought. *One more and we'll quit.*

He looked around and saw a touchrue some twenty paces away, half hidden behind a large shagneedle bush. As he started toward it, Kuma suddenly raised her head.

"Did you hear that?" she asked.

"Hear what?"

"It sounded like . . ." Her voice trailed off, and she held up her hand.

This time Raffa heard it: a small chirrup.

"It's Twig!" Kuma exclaimed. "But where—"

A young raccoon dashed out from under the big shag-needle, chirping in obvious delight. Then the bush itself began to move, shaking violently, even though there was no wind.

It wasn't a bush at all: It was Roo!

The big bear's snorts and chuffs were clearly laughter as she uncurled herself, got to all fours, and lolloped over to Kuma.

"You—you wobbler!" Kuma exclaimed, greeting Roo with a thorough neck-scratching. She turned to Raffa. "That was amazing. It was actually Twig who taught her to play hide-and-seek. But it's always Twig who hides, and then Roo finds her. I've never seen Roo hide before."

"She's too big to hide," Raffa pointed out. "I mean, just now she was hiding in plain sight."

Kuma laughed. "You were playing Freeze, weren't you, Roo? Clever bear!"

Raffa knew that ever since Kuma was a young child she and Roo had spent countless days together in the

Forest. The bear had shown the girl many woodland secrets—lush berry patches, springy beds of heather, the best climbing trees. In return, Kuma had taught Roo how to avoid trouble around humans.

Now she explained. "We practiced different ways for her to stay clear of other people. I taught her to roar on cue—we made it a game. We'd take turns. I'd roar and then she'd roar, and we'd try to get louder every time."

Raffa had to smile at the image of Kuma and Roo roaring at each other. He wondered if anyone had ever heard them. *Maybe that's what started the rumors of giant bears.* Bears in the Forest were a rarity, and Raffa had never before known of one the size of Roo.

"I never actually used that tactic," Kuma said, "because I didn't want to scare anyone. Mostly we used what I call Freeze. If there were ever other people nearby, I'd say, 'Freeze, Roo!' She crouches down and stays that way—sometimes for a long time, until I tell her it's safe to move again. That's what she was doing just now, and I didn't—"

She stopped abruptly and stared at Raffa with her mouth open.

"What is it?" he asked.

She closed her mouth and swallowed. "I've got it," she said. "I think I know how we can use her against the guards."

While clipping thorns from the last touchrue, they discussed Kuma's idea at length.

"It will only work at night," she said.

"We can do what we need to do, and if the attack does happen at night, we'll be ready. We should talk it over with the council."

Thorn-collection finally completed, they took a short break. Kuma had brought squares of fried mush; Raffa still had some dried tomatoes. Roo found a hollow in the ground and settled into it for a nap. When Twig tried to get into the hollow with her, Roo swatted her out, gently but firmly.

Twig mewled pitifully and paced back and forth. Roo grunted, then rolled over so her back was to the raccoon.

Raffa found Twig's little cries heartrending. "What's the matter?" he asked anxiously. "Why won't Roo let her in?"

Kuma was watching with interest, but didn't seem the least bit perturbed. "Twig isn't a baby anymore," she said. "Roo is trying to teach her that she needs to start being independent."

"Oh." That made sense, but Raffa still didn't like seeing Twig upset.

The raccoon made one more attempt, settling herself right on top of Roo's head. Roo sat up, growling low in her throat. It was a comical sight, the huge bear with the raccoon clinging to her head and neck, but Roo's growl was never anything to laugh at.

Raffa watched as Roo pulled an unwilling Twig off her head and dropped her on the ground. He turned to Kuma, and said, "They've just given me another idea. To go with yours."

CHAPTER EIGHTEEN

I
T was late morning by the time they got back to camp, Kuma carrying Twig on her shoulder. Raffa kept thinking about everything that needed to be done. The thorns had to be soaked in nettle essence. The knitted sacks had to be finished and filled. Yet another council meeting, to present their idea for Roo . . .

And the whistles. I keep forgetting about them. We need to make a whole bunch of them.

It's too much. I'll never get it all done, we'll never be ready. And even if I get everything done, the problem is bigger than that. If everyone is too scared and can't bring themselves to do what needs doing, nothing else will matter.

His breath shortened; he found that he was almost gasping for air.

As they entered the clearing, Elson was the first person they met. He greeted Kuma with a hug, then looked at Raffa with a frown.

"What's the matter?" he asked. "Are you unwell?"

"No," Raffa said. "I'm just— There's so much to do, I don't know—" He had to force the words out one at a time.

"Put your hands on your knees, son," Elson said. "Head down."

Raffa shrugged. "It's okay—I'm all right—"

"Not asking you," Elson said, kindly but sternly. "Go on. Five breaths, deep ones—in through your nose, out through your mouth."

Raffa liked and respected Elson too much to disobey, even though he thought the command a waste of time.

He was wrong. By the end of the third breath, his head had already cleared and steadied. *No more panicking,* he told himself firmly. *The only way to get everything done is to do one thing at a time.*

When he straightened up, he saw Elson gazing at him intently.

"Thanks," Raffa said, with a small wave. Elson nodded and patted his shoulder.

Raffa turned to Kuma. "Will you tell him about your idea for Roo? I need to get these thorns to the pother tent."

"An idea for Roo?" Elson said, with a smile. "I like the sound of that."

Raffa poured the nettle essence into the buckets holding the thorns. He gave the thorns a good stir with a wooden paddle; they would steep and become thoroughly saturated. He covered the bucket with a cloth and set it aside.

Then he joined Garith and Jimble, who were transferring the blue-goo—which was what Jimble had christened it—into smaller jars. With the three of them working together, it didn't take long. Raffa had the last jar in his hand when Jimble turned his head toward the tent door.

"What's that?" he asked.

Raffa heard what sounded like a distant clowder of cats and kittens, mewing, meowing, yowling. He nudged

Garith and touched his own ear.

They all went outside. The noise continued, coming closer, although Raffa still couldn't see anything.

"What do you hear?" Garith asked.

Raffa shook his head. "It sounds like cats"—he put his hand near his face and tweaked invisible whiskers—"but that can't be right."

"Oh!" Jimble exclaimed. "I can hear Camma and Cassa!"

He took off running. Raffa and Garith followed him. When they turned the corner onto the central path through the camp, Raffa saw the source of the noise.

A ragged flock of small children was making its way through the camp. Almost all of the children were crying pitifully, which was why, from a distance, they had sounded like cats. There were several dozen of them being shepherded by three adults and five teenagers, including Jimble's friend Davvis. Raffa recognized one of the adults, Mannum Abdul, whom he had met earlier at Kuma's settlement.

By the time Raffa and Garith caught up with Jimble, he was down on one knee, surrounded by his tearful siblings. Camma and Cassa clung to either shoulder, while toddler Brid held on to the front of Jimble's tunic. Davvis was there, too.

"What's going on?" Raffa asked.

Jimble looked at him over Camma's head. "They're taking all the little ones to one of the settlements. To keep them safe."

Davvis spoke up. "My mam said I had to help take them there. But I'm coming back after they're all steadied."

Raffa surveyed the group quickly. It looked as though every young child was leaving. At some point, Kuma had mentioned the council's decision: children under twelve to be moved to the settlements; twelve- to sixteen-year-olds would assist around camp. Only those over sixteen would be assigned to battle squads.

Jimble was ten.

"Do you need anything?" Raffa asked. "We can run and fetch it for you."

Jimble looked puzzled. "Why would I need anything?"

"I meant, to take with you."

"Take with—" Jimble stopped. A dark scowl appeared on his usually sunny face. "Oh no. No, no, nooooooo. You think I'm leaving? Faults and fissures, never in a hundred years! No, a thousand! No, a *million*!"

Raffa was saved from having to respond by the twins, who immediately began to clamor.

"Jimble, you're coming with us, right?"

"You have to come!"

"We won't go without you."

"That's right. We won't go unless you come."

"Look at me, I'm sitting down." Cassa sat down in the dirt. "I'm sitting down and I'm not getting up until you come with us."

"Me, too," Camma said, "I'm sitting down, too. And so is Brid."

She tugged on Brid's arm. The little boy lost his balance and started to fall, but Jimble caught him before he hit the ground. Brid thought it was a game. He stopped crying and clapped his hands. "More!" he said.

Raffa had encountered Jimble's younger sisters and brother once before, when he had found himself just as bewildered as he was now. An only child, he was utterly unaccustomed to multiple siblings. It was hard for him to believe that there were just three little Marrs; he would have sworn from the clamor they created that there were at least ten of them.

Jimble seemed oblivious to the noise and spoke right

over the top of it. "You can't make me leave. Only my da could do that, and—and maybe Trixin. And they're not here."

Raffa thought for a moment. On the one hand, Jimble was right. Raffa did not have any real authority to order him around. At the same time, Raffa felt responsible for him: Trixin had sent Jimble to help him more than once, always on the condition that Raffa keep him out of trouble. He decided to try an appeal to Jimble's own sense of responsibility.

"You're right, Jimble," Raffa said. "They're not here, which makes you the oldest. The one who has to make the decisions. When you left Gilden, your da and Trixin—they told you to look after the little ones, didn't they?"

Jimble stuck out his bottom lip and said nothing, which Raffa took as a sign that he was on the right track.

"How are you going to do that, if you don't go with them now?"

"You just said that I'm the one who gets to make the decisions," Jimble countered, his eyes narrowing.

Caught out, Raffa scowled. "Yes, but only if you make the *right* ones," he muttered. *If he doesn't leave, and—and something happens to him, it would be too* awful. And Trixin will—what's that she always says?— she'll skin me alive.

"You don't understand," Jimble said. "I look after them every single day. Those times in Gilden when I helped you—those were practically the only times I ever got to do anything without them. And now I have another chance, and—and it's not just fun, it's *important*, and you can't make me go!"

Raffa was taken aback by Jimble's outburst. He didn't know what to say. He looked at Garith, who was studying their faces carefully.

Garith pulled Raffa aside. "I didn't follow every-thing," he said, "but you think he should go and he doesn't want to, right?"

Raffa nodded.

"I know leaving would be safer for him," Garith said, "but he's a big help with the pothering. He listens good, and he's got a knack for it. We'll need him."

Still undecided, Raffa looked around. The rest of the group had moved on ahead. At the rear, he saw Man-num Abdul turn and walk back toward them, with a determined, no-nonsense expression on his face.

"I'll look after him," Garith went on. "You have to meet with people and talk to them and all that. I'll be staying in the pother tent; I'll keep him with me. He'll be safe enough there."

Raffa sighed. It seemed too big a decision for him and Garith to make, but at least they were making it together.

By now Mannum Abdul had reached the Marr siblings. Jimble handed over Brid. But Camma was still hanging on to one of Jimble's legs, and Cassa the other.

"We have to get going," Mannum Abdul said. "The wagons are ready to leave."

Raffa pointed at Jimble. "He's staying."

"Oh?" Abdul frowned. "I don't know—"

"We need his help with the pothering," Garith said.

Jimble's eyes lit up with surprise and thanks. "Yes, that's right," he said, squaring his shoulders. "I'm helping out in the pother tent."

Mannum Abdul nodded. "Steady work to the three of you, then," he said. "We're all counting on you."

He hoisted Brid onto his shoulders. Jimble pulled Camma to her feet, then turned to do the same to Cassa. The second he let go of Camma, she sat down and grabbed his leg again.

Jimble groaned in frustration.

Cassa stopped in midwail. "Jimble, what's that on

your hand?" She had spotted the smear of blue-goo, which was still glowing.

Of course, Camma had to see it, too, which meant that she also stopped crying. "It's a blue light," she said to Cassa.

"A pretty blue light," Cassa agreed. "I want one."

"Me, too," Camma said. "I want a blue light on my hand."

Then Raffa remembered that he had left the pother tent holding a jar of blue-goo, which he had put in his pocket at some point. He pulled it out and held it up before the twins.

"Camma and Cassa, if I give you a blue light, will you go with Davvis?"

The girls looked at each other.

"No," they said in unison.

Raffa sighed. *I was sure it would work—I'll never understand little kids. . . .*

"Two," Camma said.

"Two *each*," Cassa said.

Does that mean—?

"Okay," Jimble said. "Say it, Camma."

"Two blue lights and we'll go with Davvis," Camma said.

"Cassa?"

"No, don't ask her. I said it for both of us," Camma said.

"I don't want you to," Cassa objected. "I want to say it myself."

"Oh, for quake's sake, then say it!" Jimble exclaimed.

"Okay, okay," Cassa grumbled, then paused. "What am I supposed to say again?"

Davvis and Mannum Abdul shouted with laughter, which set everyone else laughing, too. Raffa rubbed blue-goo on the backs of the twins' hands and on one of Brid's. They hugged and kissed Jimble good-bye and finally departed, waving their glowing blue hands in front of them.

"Shakes and tremors!" Raffa said.

Jimble grinned. "That was easy," he said. "You should see when they put up a fuss."

CHAPTER NINETEEN

RAFFA organized a meeting at the pother tent: Jimble and Garith; Kuma and Twig; Callian and Bando. The raccoons were kept busy with a handful of walnuts each.

Raffa began by listing the tactics and their progress in preparation. "We still need more knitted sacks. There's a meeting this afternoon so I can show everyone how to use them. As far as *when* they get used, that will be up to Missum Quellin and Mannum Fitzer and whoever else is in command of the battle squads."

"Raffa." Garith was frowning. "You know that

people aren't going to like it, right? How are you going to convince them?"

Raffa shook his head. "It's not like there are a lot of choices. I think they'll understand that."

Garith shrugged. "I hope so."

Next on the list: The touchrue thorns soaked in nettle essence had to be distributed.

"Jimble, we're going to need locuster pods—the big ones, lots of them. That's the only way I can think of for everyone to carry a supply of the thorns without getting stung themselves. You'll need to collect at least a few hundred and hand them round."

"Got it," Jimble said. "Hundreds, collect them, hand them round. I'll have it done before you blink. What's a locuster pod?"

Raffa, Kuma, and Garith all rolled their eyes.

"City snicker," Raffa teased. Trixin had called him and Kuma "country lumpkins" in the past when they had been confused by life in Gilden; he wished she were here now to experience the reverse.

"I'll show you," Garith said. "I saw a stand of locuster trees near the stable area. There should be plenty of pods there."

After further discussion, it was agreed that Jimble should take a wheelbarrow to collect the pods, then load the buckets of thorns on it as well and take it around the camp. People would fill the pods with thorns themselves, which would save time and trouble. "I'll be sure to tell them to wear gloves," Jimble said. He was obviously relishing being part of the team.

Garith and Jimble departed, heading for the locuster trees. That left Callian and Kuma.

"Callian, we have an idea for another battle tactic," Raffa said. "Believe it or not, we're going to use Twig."

The three humans looked at the raccoons, both dozing after their walnut feast. Bando was curled up beneath Callian's feet, surrounded by broken nutshells. Twig was draped over the end of one of the logs. She was so relaxed, Raffa couldn't figure out why she didn't roll right off.

"Hmm," Callian said. "She doesn't exactly look battle-ready, does she?"

Raffa and Kuma both laughed.

"It's getting on for sunfall," Kuma said in Twig's defense. "They'll both be livelier soon enough."

"We were wondering if maybe Bando could be a part of it, too," Raffa said.

Callian peered down at Bando. When he looked up again, his face was thoughtful.

"I'm guessing you wouldn't be putting them in any danger," he said.

"No." Kuma shook her head firmly. "They'll be nowhere near the actual fighting—if there is any. But we're probably going to need your help. Roo is part of the plan, too, and Twig is used to her. But Bando isn't, so he might need some persuading."

"Ah, that name again," Callian said. "When will I get to meet the mysterious Roo?"

"I can take you to meet her," Kuma said with a shy smile. "Later today, if you want."

"Make sure she's in the right kind of mood first," Raffa added. "If she's not, I wouldn't go anywhere near her—she can be pretty ferocious."

"Shakes, you're making her sound like—like a bear or something," Callian said.

Raffa and Kuma exchanged puzzled glances.

"You didn't tell him?" Raffa asked.

Kuma frowned a little. "I guess it never came up," she said.

"What never came up?" Callian was clearly confused.

"She *is* a bear," Kuma said.

Callian shrugged. "Some folks are just grumpier than others, I guess."

Raffa snorted. "No, she's a *bear*. A really big one." He stretched his arm overhead to indicate Roo's height.

Callian looked at Raffa. "A bear."

Raffa nodded.

Callian turned to Kuma. "A bear?"

"A bear," she said.

"Um, are you—is she—"

"A bear," they said together.

A pause.

"Okay," Callian said at last. "A bear."

Kuma thought it would be easier to work with the raccoons later in the day, when they were more alert. So they went on to the next thing on Raffa's list: carving willow whistles.

The three of them walked to the stream to find willow trees. They located a small grove right away, and cut several twigs to the correct size. Raffa showed Callian how to slash the mouthpiece at an angle, and how to carve the bark in a circle so it could be loosened and removed.

Sitting on a stream bank, carving willow whistles on a spring afternoon . . . It should have been the most idyllic of tasks. But thinking of what lay ahead of them, Raffa was grim and unsmiling. He was also whittling poorly. Whittling, he realized, was one of those skills best accomplished with your hands full and your mind pleasantly empty.

Still, it was a space of time in which to think, which it seemed like he hadn't had since leaving the Garrison. And a chance to talk to Callian.

"Will you tell me about my mam?" Raffa asked. "About what she's trying to do, with your da—I mean, the Advocate?"

Callian put down his knife and the whistle he was working on. "My da has tendants with him day and night," he said. "He never used to. But the Chancellor says he needs them now, because he's not himself. He hasn't left his quarters for ages. And for the last few weeks no one's been able to see him privately. Including me."

His face was tight with worry. "Somehow, your mam will have to get in to see him and treat him with whatever will fix him. Without anyone else knowing about it. And then she'll have to get him away from his tendants to bring him here."

Raffa swallowed. It sounded dangerous for both his mam and Callian's da. "She has people helping her, right?"

Callian nodded. "I already told you about Penyard, the ferry rower. And your friend Trixin. And there's an old tendant who's been with my da for years, Bakama. He's retired now, but he'd do anything for my da. I introduced him to your mam before I left Gilden."

"Trixin," Kuma said. "Whatever I was doing, I'd want her on my side." She gave Raffa an encouraging smile.

And there's Da, Raffa thought. *I escaped from the Garrison, so maybe he can, too. Mam and Da—together, they could do it. I know they could.*

Callian picked up his whittling again, and they were all quiet for a while. Then another question popped out of Raffa's mouth, almost before his mind had formed the thought.

"Why?" he asked. "Why does the Chancellor want to get rid of all the Afters?" He didn't even know who he was asking.

He tried to answer his own question. "She said . . . in that speech she gave, she said she wants to get rid of—of blight and ugliness. She seemed to be talking about the slums, but I think what she really meant was the people. The Afters."

"My da has talked to me about this," Callian said. "Not this exactly—he doesn't know what she's doing now—but anyway . . . He says it's natural for people to want to stick with their own. Animals do the same thing. But we're supposed to be better than animals— you know, smarter and nobler and all that."

A pause. Raffa was listening intently.

"It's not hard to care about people who are like you," Callian continued. "Your own family, and people like them. But my da says we have to always make the extra effort with people who *aren't* like us. To care about them and listen to them, *especially* if they're different from us. Because that's one of the things that makes us human. It's something we can do that other animals can't."

Callian's words were making a lot of sense to Raffa. "But it's easier not to," he said slowly. "She's counting on that, on there being lots of people who—who don't want to try."

"Or maybe don't know that they should," Kuma added quietly.

Raffa thought of those who had chanted with such venom during the Chancellor's speech, and his stomach felt as cold as snowmelt. *Even if we win . . . if all the Afters stay, there will still be a lot of work to do.*

"Lunch!" Jimble announced, holding up a huge basket.

The group had reconvened at the pother tent for sun-peak meal. "I thought it would save time if I brought it here. I wasn't sure what to get, so I just told the food people that it was for the pothers, and you should see what they gave us!"

Raffa and Garith almost knocked heads looking into the basket. An entire pan of skillet bread. Boiled eggs. Cheese. Dried plums and dried apples. Bramble jam and honeycomb. A waterskin of sweet cider.

"Is that butter?" Raffa picked up a small jar covered with muslin. "Where in the world did they get butter? And eggs?"

"People from the farmsteads keep coming by and bringing stuff," Jimble said. "Some are going to fight alongside us. Even though they're not Afters."

"Did you tell them it was for five people?" Raffa said. "This looks like an awful lot of food."

"I said it was for the pothers, and Missum Tevin—I know her from the slums—she said, 'Fill it up. They'll need strength to do their magic.' And then people were saluting me and patting me on the back and all, like I was famous or something!"

Raffa's stomach juddered. *It wasn't me, Da—honest! I swear I never said a word about magic!*

His thoughts had gone straight to his father, who had always detested any hint that apothecary involved magic, or that pothers were magicians. Here in camp, the slum dwellers, like most other city folk, knew little or nothing of plants and botanicals; to them, the art of apothecary was a mystery wrapped in a riddle. Raffa realized that he should have been prepared for the question of magic to arise.

Mohan's greatest vitriol was reserved for those who sought apothecary solutions for impossible wishes, which were known among pothers as *yearnings*. People who came to Mohan seeking a botanical combination for, say, effortless wealth or instant beauty were chased from the house with such fury that they never dared return.

But Raffa also knew that both his parents hoped one day to be able to devote time to another kind of yearning: the heartrending desire for cures for incurable illnesses. In that moment, he understood something he had never quite grasped before.

People with the deepest kinds of yearnings want to believe in magic because they're afraid. Of sickness or dying . . . or losing their loved ones. The folks here are afraid that the Chancellor will win, and drive them out of Obsidia for good. And they think only magic can save them.

Raffa shook his head. Hard work, inspiration, cooperation—those things so often produced incredible results. Unexpected, amazing, and yes, magical results.

Why did so many people think that magic was better than magical?

CHAPTER TWENTY

RAFFA stood at the center of the semicircle of stumps. On the ground at his side was his rucksack, which contained, among other things, several knitted sacks filled with the antidote powder.

Before him sat the five members of the council. Standing behind the council were almost a hundred people, both Afters and settlers, who had been chosen to serve as squad leaders for the upcoming battle. Raffa had never spoken to so many people at the same time. He swallowed hard, wishing he had asked one of his friends to come with him. But Kuma and Callian were busy training the raccoons, while Jimble and Garith continued their work at the pother tent, filling more of the little sacks.

The squad leaders had checked in earlier, with a roll call.

"Kettle Squad."

"Drainpipe Squad, ready."

"Bucket Squad here."

The squad leaders had decided amongst themselves that their squads would be named after ordinary household items. The idea was that the ninety-eight squad names put together would list everything needed for a family's home. "Because," one of them had explained to the council, "that's what we're fighting for."

There was Window Squad and Door Squad; Wall Squad and Roof Squad; Hearth Squad and Stove Squad. The Attic and Basement Squad leaders were sister and brother. Every item of kitchenware you could think of was represented, as were tools, household linens, clothing. Raffa's particular favorites were the Pincushion Squad, the Soap Squad, and the Woolen-Sock Squad.

The squad leaders knew how rare smiles were around the camp. As they had intended, it was hard to think of the squad names without an occasional smile.

Elson had told Raffa that everyone present knew

the essential background about the animals: They were being dosed with a botanical combination that made them easy to train, and they had been trained to attack people. Raffa stood up as straight as he could.

"First, I want to tell you about the antidote," he said. His voice wobbled in the middle of the sentence, but he forced himself to continue. "We've made it into a powder. We know it works when it's *fed* to animals, but that takes too long to go through their systems."

He already felt less nervous. I know this stuff, he thought.

"The fastest way for a botanical combination to take effect is if it's inhaled," he continued. "It's pretty much instant—it gets into the bloodstream immediately."

He bent down to reach into his rucksack. "The sacks that everyone has been knitting," he said as he held up a pair in front of him, "have been filled with antidote powder. The idea is to get the animals to bite into a sack. It will sort of explode right in their faces, and they'll inhale the powder. As soon as they do, they'll return to their natural, undosed state, which means that they'll be afraid of humans. *All* humans. They won't listen to the guards anymore—they'll just run off."

He pointed to one of the sack's "sausages."

"We've tied them off in sections. That way, when one part gets bitten, the powder doesn't all spill out. And there are two more sections, for two more animals."

A man standing behind Quellin raised his hand. "I'm Brick Squad. This sounds clever and all. But how do we get the beasts to bite the sacks?"

Raffa took a breath to steady himself. This was the hard part. The council had already approved the idea, but only after a long and labored discussion. Raffa knew he had to do more than just present the plan to the squad leaders: He had to gain their support and enthusiasm.

"The animals they're using are mostly foxes and stoats," he said. "Some badgers, but not as many. The badgers stay low to the ground. They attack by trying to bite people's ankles, tripping them up. The foxes and stoats have been trained to—to jump into the air and go for people's throats."

The squad leaders immediately began talking.

"That's right—that's what happened at the river crossing."

"Jonno got bit on the shoulder. The beast was going for his throat, sure upon certain."

"The stoats at the settlement—they jumped for the chickens on their roosts."

Haddie twisted in her seat to face the audience behind her, her hand raised. She didn't say a word, but everyone quieted. Then she turned back and nodded at Raffa.

Raffa took the two knitted sacks he was holding, looped them around his neck, and tied them.

"We wear them like this," he said. "Like a collar. When the animals attack, we stand as still as we can, and expose our necks fully, so they'll jump and bite right through the wool."

He knew it was a lot to ask. But it was also their best chance at getting the animals to inhale the antidote.

The buzz began again, only this time it was more like a roar.

"You mean, I'm to *let* them jump and—and tear at me?"

"You can't be serious!"

"Are you quake-brained? That's impossible!"

Elson stood and shouted over the noise. "Ears!" he said, his voice not so much loud as deep and sonorous. When the talk subsided, he asked, "Raffa, can't we just figure out a way to release the powder into the air, like— like snow?"

Raffa shook his head. "That's not direct enough. Some of the animals might not inhale very much, and others might not get any at all."

"How about hitting them on the noses with those sacks?" Quellin suggested.

"That would be better," Raffa said, "but what if the sack doesn't burst? This"—he pointed to his own neck—"is the surest way we could think of to make certain they get a good solid whiff of the antidote. It's using their own strength against them."

"Let them *snap at our throats*?" A woman clutched her neck. "I can't go back to my squad and ask them to do that!"

Raffa spoke quickly. "Everyone should wear two," he said, "one on top of the other. It would be hard for the animals to bite through both and get to—to someone's skin. And we've got shorter ones to tie around our ankles and wrists."

But hardly anyone heard him; they had all begun talking at once. Raffa could hear their alarm; his cheeks burned from the heat of their protests. Standing there in front of the group, he felt his heart beating faster and his breath becoming ragged.

If they won't do this—if I can't convince them— then the animals and the guards will drive us all the way to the Suddens. The Chancellor will win. And it will be my fault.

As the crowd's unrest continued, his hopelessness grew. *I don't blame them. Hardly any of them know me. Why should they trust me? I'm just a kid talking about apothecary, which they don't even understand—*

A desperate idea took shape in his mind, and he spoke before he could think even a second longer.

"Hoy!" he called out. "Listen, I haven't told you everything yet!"

Elson called again for quiet. Everyone complied, but Raffa could still sense their fear simmering below the silence.

"So, um, the powder?" he said. "It has special powers. Like I said, it will cure the animals, but it also—it does—I mean, it can—"

"Speak up!" shouted a man at the back. "Can't hear you!"

Raffa's desperate impulse seemed to have taken on a life of its own: He couldn't stop now; he had to plunge on. He cleared his throat, almost choking on what he was about to say. "These collars," he said, and pointed to them again, "they—they can protect whoever's wearing them."

"The collars?" The same voice, incredulous.

"No, no, sorry," Raffa said hastily. "Not the collars—the powder. The powder inside them, it's really—um, special. It's made from a rare plant, one that no one's ever seen before." That part, at least, was true, and his voice gained strength. "It has powers that—that no one else knows about." *Also true,* he told himself fiercely.

"Magic!" someone cried out.

The word rippled through the crowd.

Magic.

A magic plant.

It will protect us.

Fearful expressions began to smooth out and were replaced by curiosity, even eagerness.

"You hear that?" the man at the back called out. "We'll be protected—the beasts can't hurt us!"

"What about weapons?" Another voice. "Does it protect against weapons, too?"

"Knives, I'll wager—they're like a beast's teeth."

Excitement spread throughout the group, and Raffa saw hope gleaming in people's eyes.

Someone shouted, "Cheers to the young pother, then!"

"Raffa. His name's Raffa!"

"Raffa—Raffa—Raffa—"

Now they were all chanting his name. Raffa stood in wide-eyed surprise, which the group seemed to take as modesty. They cheered even louder.

"RAFFA! RAFFA! RAFFA!"

He bowed over his clasped hands in a gesture of appreciation. Inside, he was still stunned—and jittery with excitement as well.

This was exactly what we needed.

The display of hope and enthusiasm he saw before him could carry them all the way to victory!

CHAPTER TWENTY-ONE

R AFFA left the meeting with his cheeks flushed, feeling almost giddy. The gloom over the whole camp had lifted. For the first time, people seemed excited rather than afraid.

"Going down to the stream, Raffa?"

"Blowpipe practice—come watch us."

They were strangers, squad leaders he didn't know, but now they all felt like they knew him.

"I can't stay long," he said, "but I'd love to take a quick look."

Down by the stream, squad leaders shouted instructions.

"Floorboards! Look lively now!"

"Keep it up, Trowel Squad!"

"Faster, Pillows, faster!"

Every squad had twelve members. Five squads at a time lined up streamside, in ranks of four. Each rank blew thorns—ordinary ones, from hawberry trees—into the stream repeatedly, until their pipes were empty. Then they split into pairs, peeling off right and left to allow the next quartet to step forward. While awaiting their turns, they reloaded their pipes.

The Afters seemed both determined and good-humored. They called out encouragement to one another, laughed off the stumbles, and worked without cease. Their movements were shakes and tremors at first. But after several rounds of repetition, the action smoothed out and began to look almost like a dance.

If only it were a dance, Raffa thought.

Farther upstream, accuracy practice was taking place. The council had speculated that the guards would not be wearing heavy armor, for two reasons: because the Chancellor knew that the Afters lacked weaponry, and because, with the battle taking place in the Mag and the Forest, the guards would need to be quick and agile. But they would still be well protected by layers of leather and padding.

"Hands!" The squad leaders were calling out. "First choice, hit them in the hand. Second choice, face or neck." These were the places where the thorns had the best chance to penetrate unprotected flesh.

To Raffa's astonishment, squad members began setting up a few dozen scarecrows in a long line, their poles planted in the shallow water at the stream's edge. The last time he had seen scarecrows was at the shed compound, where they were being used to train the crows—to peck out people's eyes.

The squad members were now blowing darts at the scarecrows. Raffa could not help an involuntary shudder at the similarity between what he was seeing now and what he had seen at the shed compound.

A sober realization: War made both sides alike in frightening ways.

Raffa left the stream bank. He meant to head for the pother tent, but his feet took him toward the outskirts of the clearing. He began to jog, slowly at first, then faster and faster, until he found himself barreling through the Forest. He plunged on blindly, branches whipping at his face and catching his sleeves. He did not know how long he had been running when he saw an enormous never-bare tree with a hollowed-out trunk.

He veered off the path, then headed straight for the tree and ducked into its hollow. Pulling the hood of his tunic over his head, he made himself as small as he could by hugging his knees.

Slowly the wild pounding of his heart began to ease.

What had happened?

The scarecrows. It was something about seeing the scarecrows, and the thought that both sides were using them.

The image in Raffa's mind shifted. He saw himself at the center of the circle, speaking to the council and all the squad leaders.

They were cheering for me! So exciting . . . and everyone so hopeful . . .

But his body had known the truth just now, and had made him run away—in shame.

A few thoughtless words had exploded into a dreadful fraud. He had *lied* to all those people.

Just like the Chancellor, who had been lying all

along. Saying she wanted animals trained to do the work of people; giving away grain as a means of ferreting out all the Afters; claiming that her plan was to raze the slums . . .

Well, he was no better. He had lied to people who were depending on him. Not only that, but his mistake was grounded in a cowardly yearning: the wish to make a difficulty vanish without effort.

But I never said it! I never said the word magic, *it was someone else—*

Now he was making things worse by trying to justify what he had done. He cringed at the thought of how his parents would react if they knew.

If everyone thinks they're protected by magic, they might do really foolish things. They won't take care to protect themselves.

His mistake might end up getting more people hurt or even killed. Why hadn't he thought of that before? Tears filled his eyes and rolled down his cheeks—tears of rage at himself mixed with tears of self-pity. It was surely one of the most awful combinations in the world.

If only Echo were still with him! The little bat would have comforted him, and probably even made him laugh. He recalled the many times he had been puzzled or troubled, and just being with Echo had helped him solve the problem.

His forehead on his knees, Raffa thought about his conversations with the bat. He always had to choose words that Echo would understand, which usually meant explaining complicated situations in basic terms. He would slow things down and simplify them—and it was then that a solution would come to him.

I know exactly what Echo would say if he were here now. He'd say, "Raffa no good?"

"That's right, Echo," he whispered. "I—I told a lie. To a whole lot of people. Many people."

Did Echo know all those words? *No, so he might say, "Lie? What lie?"*

"A lie is—is when you don't tell the truth."

"What truth?"

"Truth? Truth is—well, it's the way things are."

No. That wasn't quite right. Because, Raffa thought, there isn't just one way. *People see the same thing in different ways. Sometimes even in opposite ways. What's bad to one person might be good, or at least okay, to someone else. Like the Chancellor. Dosing the animals and using them against people—somehow, she sees it as a good thing. . . .*

So you had to try to look at the world as clearly as you could. But that alone wasn't enough: You also had to measure what you saw against what you thought was right. *The truth isn't just facts. It's feelings, too.*

"Truth, Echo . . . Truth is seeing the world with both your mind and your heart."

Raffa had been thinking so hard that he felt like his brain was getting sore. He knew how he wanted this imaginary conversation to end: He wanted to hear Echo say, "Raffa good!"

He would have to earn it first.

For the next hour or so, Raffa made birchbark masks. First he walked through the Forest, locating birch trees. He cut the bark, always careful not to take too much from any one tree. When he had gathered a large stack of bark, he sat down on a log, trimmed the pieces into squares, and cut eye slits and "fake" eyeholes into each square.

He knew that he should go back to the pother tent to see how Garith and Jimble were doing. But after what had just happened, he needed this time in the Forest for succor and strength. And there were bound to be some folks who hadn't had a chance to make their own masks and would need one, so at least he was still being useful.

As he worked with his hands, his mind was hard at work, too. How could he fix his dreadful mistake?

It did not take long for him to come to the conclusion that *how* was not the hard part. He knew what had to be done: The only way to undo a lie was by telling the truth . . . *and* getting people to believe it.

I'm NOT like the Chancellor. She thinks it's okay to lie. I know that what I did was wrong, and I have to fix it.

The hard part was when and where. And to whom.

He tried out various scenarios. *I could tell the council. Or—or just one or two of them. Fitzer, maybe?*

Then what? Leave it to the council to tell everyone else?

No. That would be putting one act of cowardice on top of another.

I could go around telling the squad leaders one by one. That way I wouldn't have to stand up in front of a whole bunch of people again.

Another no. There wasn't enough time.

Only one solution had the best chance of succeeding, but the thought of it made Raffa queasy with fear. *Please, please let me think of something else—and soon. . . .*

Finally he could delay no longer, and walked slowly back to camp. He was relieved to find the pother tent empty when he arrived; it was time for the evening meal, so Garith and Jimble were probably at the pavilion.

The tent looked almost forlorn. In contrast to the constant activity of the past two days, the worktable had been cleared, with empty basins and buckets underneath. The piles of knitted and filled collars, the touchrue thorns, and the jars of blue-goo were all gone; everything had been distributed throughout the camp. One basket held a few birchbark masks; he added the ones he had made.

Garith and Jimble had worked hard and heroically. Nearly everything was ready.

Raffa couldn't face seeing everyone at the pavilion, not yet. He found the lunch basket, which contained some leftovers. He ate the rest of the skillet bread with some cheese and jam. Then he went to Haddie and Elson's tent.

Haddie came out when he called.

"I need to arrange another meeting," Raffa said.

"The council?" she asked. "Or the squad leaders?"

He gulped. "No," he said, forcing out the next words. "The whole camp." By now, most if not all of the leaders would have passed the lie on to their squad members. It was his responsibility to make sure that *everyone* knew the truth.

She didn't bat an eye. "That'll be easy enough," she said. "The council is going to address the camp tonight, at moonrise. You can say your piece there."

Raffa's stomach filled with tremors. He realized that he had been hoping she would say something like, "*The whole camp? That won't be possible.*"

It was done now. He had to figure out what he was going to say.

CHAPTER TWENTY-TWO

O N his way back to the pother tent, Raffa saw
Kuma and the two raccoons up ahead of him
on the path. He called to her.

"How did it go with them?" he asked, nodding at the
raccoons.

"Couldn't have gone better," she said. "They think
it's a game. Twig trusts Roo completely—she doesn't bat
an eye. Bando was a little skittish at first, but he followed Twig's lead." She grinned. "You should see him.
He closes his eyes really tight the whole time."

Raffa squatted down and smiled at the twins. Twig

began trying to untie one of his bootlaces while Bando pawed at the dirt beside the path. "Where's Callian?"

No answer. He glanced up to see a worried expression on Kuma's face.

"He left," she said at last. "He's on his way back to Gilden."

"*What?* Why?"

"He said he has to help rescue his father. That he realized he never should have left him in the first place, except for having to deliver the message from Salima."

"But that's just reckless—he might end up getting caught himself!"

She flashed a scowl at him. "You weren't there, Raffa. I didn't even try to talk him out of it. The look in his eyes—there was no way I could have stopped him."

He held his breath for a beat. "Okay. I didn't mean— I'm not angry at *you*." Pause. "I guess I'm not really angry at him, either. I—I just hope he'll be all right."

They stood in silence for a moment. Raffa found himself wishing silently, *Find my mam and da, too, Callian. Get them all out of Gilden.*

Then Bando chittered, and trundled over to him. "Errrmmmm," the raccoon said happily. "Errrrmmmm."

Something dangled from his mouth. Raffa bent down for a closer look.

It was a fat, juicy earthworm.

Bando mistook Raffa's interest. He took the partly eaten worm out of his mouth and held it up. "Errr-mmmm?" he asked politely.

Before Raffa could refuse his generous offer, Twig loped over. She swiped the worm out of Bando's paw and swallowed it in one gulp.

It happened so quickly that Bando was completely flummoxed. He looked at his own paws, first one, then the other, squeaking in puzzlement. What had happened to his worm?

Raffa and Kuma both laughed. Bando continued to squeak until Raffa comforted him with a piece of dried apple from his rucksack.

As they reached the pother tent, Jimble and Garith joined them. Kuma decided to take the two raccoons to the stream to let them play and scrabble for crayfish.

"They worked hard—they deserve a little rest," she said.

She picked up Twig, who chirped cheerfully.

"Let me hold her?" Raffa begged. "Just for a minute."

Kuma handed over the raccoon, who was now quite an armful, not the little furball she had been when Raffa first met her. He rubbed behind her ears, then cradled her close to his face. She reached up with her humanlike hands and patted his chin and cheeks.

"Hey, Twiglet," he murmured, thinking of her future mission. "Be—be careful, okay?"

"Bee-bee kay," Twig said. "Bee-bee kay."

"I like it," Kuma said as Raffa handed Twig back to her. "Bee-bee kay, everyone."

"Bee-bee kay-one!" Bando squeaked.

"Bee-bee kay-one!" Jimble repeated, and giggled.

Raffa had to roll his eyes. What he had just heard was a human who was imitating a raccoon who was imitating a human.

Jimble went with Kuma, delighted to have a chance to play with the raccoons. That left Raffa alone with Garith for the first time in what seemed like weeks. They straddled the log outside the pother tent, facing each other. Raffa was trying hard not to think about the upcoming meeting at the pavilion.

"Garith, have you gotten used to being deaf?"

Raffa was astonished by his own words. *Where did that come from?* "Sorry. Never mind—I don't even know why I asked."

"No, it's okay," Garith said. "Nobody seems to— I mean, everybody avoids the subject. I don't ever get to talk about it."

He leaned forward, his forearms on his knees. "It's not like I think about it every single second," he said. "Sometimes I forget about it. When it doesn't matter. Like when I'm pothering. Maybe that's why I like it so much these days."

Raffa nodded slowly. "That makes sense."

"You're not gonna believe this," Garith said, "but there's even times when I'm glad."

"Really?" Raffa exclaimed, both startled and skeptical.

Garith grinned wickedly. "Think about it. If I weren't deaf, I'd probably have killed Jimble by now."

Raffa snorted. Garith jumped to his feet. He started bouncing around on his toes and doing a reasonable imitation of Jimble. "'Garith, how much of this should I put in?' 'Garith, am I stirring this right?' 'Garith, I want to do it myself—will you watch me?'"

Now Raffa was laughing, and Garith joined in. When their laughter ebbed, Garith added, "He's great, really. But I'm glad we're too busy for him to experiment. Who knows what he'd get up to!"

Raffa stood, too, and faced his cousin. "Speaking of experimenting," he said, "I put some of the cavern-plant powder aside. When all this is finished"—he gestured toward the camp—"I'm going to experiment. And try to make an antidote for you."

Garith was silent for so long that Raffa wondered if he had understood. At last he spoke. "If it's just because you feel bad about—about what happened to me—that's not . . . enough of a reason."

Another long silence. "I can't be sitting around waiting and hoping, you know what I mean? I have to—to get on with things. With my life, the way it is. But if you want to experiment because what you find out might help other people, then that's a good reason."

Raffa inhaled a quick breath. *He's talking about yearnings.* An antidote that might help a lot of people: That was a truly worthwhile yearning.

He gave Garith a mock-scowl. "When did you get so clever?"

Garith shrugged. "Always been that way, dear cousin. You just never noticed before."

They took turns jostling each other as they walked to the pavilion.

The tables had been moved out of the pavilion and replaced by benches, stumps, and logs for seating. Lanterns hung from the posts. Every available place was taken. More people stood around three sides of the pavilion. The rumble of talk was low but constant.

Quellin, Haddie, and Missum Abdul, three of the council members, stood along the fourth side, on a crude dais made of split logs. They were surrounded by the squad leaders. Raffa sat on a log near the front between Garith and Kuma, with Jimble next to Garith.

Haddie nodded at Kuma, who put her fingers to her lips, and a sharp whistle pierced the air. Most people stopped talking, but not everyone. Kuma whistled again, and this time silence filled the space all the way to its canvas roof.

The camp denizens numbered over a thousand, so the council had decided to use shouters for this gathering. For the Chancellor's speech in Gilden, there had been dozens of shouters; here, there were only two. One of them was Kuma's uncle Elson, with his beautiful basso voice; Fitzer was the other. They stood at the back of the pavilion, which put them right in the midst of the crowd.

Haddie stepped up onto a stump and greeted everyone. "Once upon a time," she said, and held up her hand.

"ONCE UPON A TIME," Elson and Fitzer yelled together.

Haddie opened both arms toward the gathering, inviting a response.

"Happily ever Afters," everyone called.

Haddie frowned. She turned her head, put one hand to her ear, and made a beckoning gesture with the other. "ONCE UPON A TIME," she repeated.

The crowd understood. "HAPPILY EVER AFTERS!" they bellowed.

She nodded, satisfied. "First, I want to thank everyone," she said.

". . . *I want to thank everyone.*" The shouters continued to echo her words.

"I know it hasn't been easy, and the way we have all worked together is truly impressive. We are most of us Afters. But whether or not you have After blood, you are here with us because you believe in fairness and justice."

After the shouters had repeated her words, applause rolled through the pavilion and spilled out its edges. Haddie waited for quiet again.

"Fairness and justice. So I would have you remember this: The guards against whom we fight are our neighbors. *And will be our neighbors again.* We seek a victory not against them but against those whose orders they follow. Fight for your families and friends, for yourselves, for Obsidia. Fight hard and well. But know that a quest for justice without wisdom and compassion can all too easily become cruelty."

"*. . . cruelty.*"

"Your squad leaders have briefed you. You know that we cannot match the guards in either numbers or weaponry. Our advantages are surprise and agility, and we *must* work together. That is where we will find our strength. So I leave you with this."

Looking to her left, she began to move her head slowly, slowly, so that her gaze swept over the entire crowd. No one spoke. The silence and stillness were majestic.

Haddie raised her hand as if to match palms with everyone there. "We are steady, together."

Elson and Fitzer repeated her words. "*We are steady, together.*"

The crowd bestirred themselves. Raffa heard a few scattered calls: "Steady, together."

Then Elson raised his voice. "STEADY!" he shouted.

Fitzer took his cue. "TOGETHER!"

Half the crowd took up Elson's cry. "STEADY!"

"TOGETHER!" answered the other half.

"STEADY!"

"TOGETHER!"

The timbers of the pavilion trembled as a thousand people clapped and stamped their feet and roared.

Haddie waited, letting the noise of the crowd ebb. At last it was quiet again.

"Many of you know Raffa Santana," she said. "He's half-After, and he's from a pother family. He has done fine work for us here, acting as camp pother, despite his young age. The squad leaders have already met him, and he would like to speak to you all now."

Raffa rose and stepped onto the dais. He put his rucksack down next to the stump, which was only a little taller than knee height. So why did it look as steep as a mountain?

His legs felt so weak, he wondered if he would be able to get onto the stump without help. He managed it, just barely. He stared down at his feet to make sure they didn't wander off the edge, then slowly raised his head.

Every single person in that enormous crowd was looking directly at him.

Raffa held his breath and tightened his stomach. *Don't throw up don't throw up don't throw up don't throw up.*

In his hand he was holding two of the knitted collars. He clutched them in a death grip.

The sooner he started talking, the sooner this would be over with. He knew what he wanted to say; he had rehearsed it in his head a hundred times.

"This afternoon," he began—and stopped. What came out of his mouth was not words, but a ragged croak. He glanced around wildly, desperate for help— and there in the crowd, he saw his friends.

Jimble, gazing up at him eagerly, looking so much like Trixin.

Kuma, her face quiet and steady.

Garith, his eyes narrowed, concentrating on reading Raffa's lips.

Suddenly Raffa noticed that his legs felt stronger: It was as if his friends were holding him upright, and even calming his roiled guts.

They were supporting him—and counting on him as well.

CHAPTER TWENTY-THREE

"T HIS afternoon I met with the council and the
squad leaders," Raffa said.

Elson and Fitzer echoed his words.

"And I—I made a mistake that I have to fix. A mistake that affects all of you."

Deep breath in. Blow it out slowly.

"As you know, these collars"—he held them up—"are
filled with a special botanical powder."

"*. . . powder.*"

"It will restore the animals to their natural state.
But—"

Here he turned a little, to look at the squad leaders

238

lined up along one side of the stump. "But that's all it does," he said, then turned the other way, toward the rest of the squad leaders. "I said it would protect us against injuries. But that's not—" He swallowed hard, then made himself speak firmly. "That's not true. It's NOT MAGIC."

". . . NOT MAGIC."

Surprise seemed to swirl through the crowd. Quickly their puzzled murmurs grew into angry shouts.

"Not magic? What's the good of pothering, then?"

"But that means there's nothing to protect us!"

"He's a liar! He lied to the squad leaders! Why should we believe him now?"

It was the hardest thing Raffa had ever done, to stand there in front of everyone while their fear and anger came pounding at him from all sides. It seemed to go on forever; he felt as if he were shrinking, getting smaller and smaller under the barrage.

Once again he looked at his friends. He saw concern on their faces . . . but also expectation.

He raised a trembling hand; the crowd quieted, although they were still seething.

"It's all my fault—not the council's, not your squad leaders'. I'm really, really sorry, but I know that being sorry isn't enough. So this is what I'm going to do, to convince you that—that we have to do this. And that it will work."

He held the collars over his head so everyone could see them, then tied them around his neck. "I'll be wearing these," he said, "and I'll stand way out front of our position. On my own. The animals will see me and attack me first. That's how sure I am that this will work, and you'll be able to see it for yourselves."

What he had just said terrified him. His only hope was that each animal had been trained to go one-on-one with a human. If a whole pack attacked him—

His stomach began rumbling again. *Stop! Stop thinking about it!*

He stared out at the throng. No one seemed to know quite what to make of his latest pronouncement; they were subdued now, but remained restless. Behind him, the council members had their heads together.

Then Haddie spoke. "The council cannot allow that," she said to Raffa. She turned toward the audience. "None of you would allow it, either. He is but a child."

A way out. She's giving me a way out.

But his next words surprised even himself.

"You can't think of me as a child," he said. "You

said it yourself: I'm the camp's head of apothecary. My parents both gave their blessing for me to do the work here. This tactic was my idea, and it's up to me to—to see it through."

It was very quiet. Raffa knew that the next moments would sway things one way or the other. *I have to say something more, while they're listening.*

"The honest truth is, no apothecary 'magic' can protect us against the guards or the animals. But look at this camp." He gestured broadly with his hands. "Look at what's been done here in just a few days! It's almost like—like a village, where there wasn't anything before. Because of everyone working together, Afters and settlers and Gildeners. Isn't that a kind of magic? The best kind?"

Elson bellowed, at the top of his lungs. "THE BEST KIND OF MAGIC!"

Jimble leapt to his feet. "The best kind of magic!" he cried out.

And Garith and Kuma stood up, too, and started chanting along with Jimble.

The best kind of magic . . . the best kind of magic . . .

Quellin stepped forward to stand next to Raffa. Haddie did the same on the other side. Each put an arm around him.

Then Fitzer changed the chant by bellowing, "STEADY TOGETHER!" He and Elson began alternating the two phrases.

STEADY TOGETHER—

THE BEST KIND OF MAGIC!

STEADY TOGETHER—

THE BEST KIND OF MAGIC!

People in the crowd were looking around. A few here and there stood and joined in. Jimble started bounding up and down the narrow aisles, waving his arms to get people to stand; those who saw him apparently couldn't resist his pleas. They stood. Others saw them and stood, too.

It wasn't long before almost everyone in the crowd was on their feet, the chant so loud it was like a wall of sound for Raffa to lean on.

Finally Haddie held up her hands for silence. Raffa nearly fell off the stump in his haste to let her take his place.

"I thought of one more thing," she said. "If you have anything leather, you can wrap a strip around your neck for extra protection." She paused for a moment. "Everyone is to have a good rest tonight. So we'll close for now."

She took a deep breath. "ONCE UPON A TIME!" she hollered.

"HAPPILY EVER AFTERS!!!" the crowd thundered back.

As the meeting broke up, people began moving stumps and logs out of the way so the tables could be put back in place. Nearly boneless with exhaustion, Raffa picked up his rucksack. He was scanning the crowd trying to find Garith when Fitzer approached him.

"What you did just now, young Santana—that was a hard thing," he said. "And you'll not stand on your own. I'm leader of Frypan Squad. The Frypans will stand with you."

Raffa's mouth fell open. He couldn't think of what to say.

"They're good folk, all of them," Fitzer went on. "Just wish I had leather for them, like Haddie said. It's not easy to come by in the slums."

A sudden inspiration hit Raffa: He opened his rucksack and took something out of it.

"This is enough leather to make collars for your whole squad," he said. He handed Fitzer a coil of rope.

His precious rope.

Which had once been a beautiful leather tunic made

by his mother, gifted him for his eleventh birthday. Without the rope, he would have been unable to harvest the scarlet vine that had healed Echo's terrible wounds. The rope had saved him from drowning in the cavern . . . and helped him escape from the secret compound. . . .

His throat thickened a little as the man took it and looked it over.

Then Fitzer untied the last segment, and gave the piece of leather to Raffa.

"You'll need that for yourself," he said, nodding.

Raffa started to thank him when he was interrupted by a shout.

"RUNNER! RUNNER IN THE CLEARING!"

Everyone stopped whatever they were doing. In that moment of pause, Elson's voice sounded throughout the pavilion.

"Council members back to the dais! Everyone else, make way for the runner!"

As if by magic, a path to the dais opened up, people stepping aside and craning their necks for a look at the runner. Raffa saw her as she entered the pavilion at a trot, her dark face shiny with sweat in the light from the lanterns. She made her way through the pavilion to the dais; the cleared path closed in behind her. Raffa thought of trying to follow, but there were too many people in the way. He spotted Kuma to his left and moved to join her.

They didn't have to wait long before they heard Elson again.

"THE FERRY ROWERS HAVE ALL BEEN CALLED IN TO WORK," he bellowed. "GUARDS CROSSING OVER TONIGHT. ATTACK AT DAY-BIRTH. . . . ATTACK AT DAYBIRTH."

It seemed to Raffa that everyone in the pavilion drew a single breath at the same moment: a thousand people in unison.

Then voices and movement burst out from all sides.

"Ladle Squad, with me!"

"Hoy, Basements!"

"Shingles, over here!"

Raffa looked at Kuma, and saw in her expression exactly what he himself was feeling: grim determination bounded by fear.

It was time.

PART III

CHAPTER TWENTY-FOUR

IN the dead of night, the whole camp seethed with urgent activity. Lanterns burned everywhere, giving the clearing an eerie look of light struggling to push away the heavy darkness. People were rushing around, not in panic but with purpose. Strangest of all, almost every single face glowed blue, the birchbark masks pushed up or down out of the way for the time being.

Raffa and Kuma hurried to the pother tent. Garith and Jimble were already there. The four friends rubbed blue-goo onto their cheeks and foreheads. They tied powder-filled sacks around their ankles and their wrists. Jimble passed out blowpipe reeds and locuster pods to each of them. Kuma had picked up one of the collars to tie around her neck when Garith stopped her.

"Wait," he said, "I've got something for you."

He pulled out three strips of leather, handed one to her and another to Jimble, and kept the third for himself. "Wrap those around your neck first," he said. He looked at Raffa. "You have your own, right?"

Raffa nodded and held up the length of leather from his rope, the one Fitzer had given him. He frowned and did a double take. "Where did you get—"

Then he saw that the bottom of Garith's leather tunic had been hacked off. Garith saw him looking and grinned. "Aunt Salima was mad at you when you cut yours up," he said. "She'll probably be *proud* of me."

Once fully dressed and equipped, the foursome gathered in a little circle. Raffa stretched his hands out toward Garith, palms together.

Garith clapped his hands around Raffa's. Jimble and Kuma joined in, too. They stood quietly for a moment. Raffa felt he should say something.

We're going off to fight. Who knows what will happen? What could I possibly say at a time like this?

It turned out to be easier than he thought. He looked

at Jimble, at Garith, at Kuma, and spoke his heart's desire.

"See you all back here in a little while."

Garith and Jimble went to meet up with Elson's squad, whom they would shadow throughout the battle. That was the compromise that had been reached, between the boys' determination to join the fight and the council's decision that no one younger than sixteen would be assigned to a squad. Raffa and Kuma left the clearing and entered the Forest. Each carried a raccoon on one arm and a lightstick in their free hand. They were going to the area where Kuma had left Roo.

Raffa had no idea how Kuma would find Roo in the vast Forest in the middle of the night, but Kuma did not seem worried in the least. After they had jog-trotted far enough for the lights and sounds of the camp to have faded behind them, she simply stopped and stood still.

"Roo!" she called. "Roo, can you hear me?"

Silence. She waited for a few moments, then called again.

Sure enough, Raffa heard snorts and snuffles and the sound of a very large animal moving through the brush.

The glow from Kuma's lightstick caught the gleam of two eyes coming toward them.

Roo and Kuma had their usual affectionate greeting, with Roo sniffing Kuma all over, and Kuma giving the great bear's neck a thorough scratch. Then Raffa gritted his teeth and stood still while Roo sniffed him between his legs. He was relieved when Roo whined in recognition.

Kuma opened the grain sack she was carrying and took out a piece of honeycomb as big as Raffa's head. "Here, Roo," she said. "Eat that up, and then we have work to do."

Now they were headed for the Mag, a vast lava field formed during the Great Quake. It was named for the magma that had been forced to the surface from deep within the earth.

According to the information garnered from the runner, the guards were using only a single river crossing, the one to the south. The crossing farther north gave directly onto the Forest of Wonders, which the guards would want to avoid as long as possible. From the ferry landing, the guards would march through the farmsteads and settlements until they reached the Mag.

The Mag's most striking features were the strange stone formations that rose from its solid basalt floor.

Some were tall, their irregular crags reaching more than twice a man's height. Others were low to the ground, pocked and rutted, with what seemed like no other purpose than to twist ankles. Many of the structures had acquired names over the years: the Poisoned Pillar, the Angry Ox, the Three-Headed Beaster.

In between those distinctive markers were pinnacles and spurs and pyramids and spires of every shape and size, making it impossible to move through the Mag in a straight line. Raffa and Kuma had to constantly divert to go around the bizarre statues of stone.

Their destination was in the area closest to the farmsteads, where the guards would first enter the Mag. There, a broad plateau of basalt began on the Mag floor and gradually sloped upward over some thirty paces, like a ramp, until it was as high as a house. Although bumpy and pitted, its top surface was more than four paces wide and fairly flat.

It was called the Bridge, although it spanned nothing and led to nowhere.

The sound rode on the night breeze, reaching Roo's ears first. She raised her head and looked toward the edge of the Mag.

Kuma saw the bear's movement. "What is it, Roo?"

The bear was sprawled on the ground at the base of the Bridge, with Raffa and Kuma leaning against her side for warmth. They were all snatching a few moments' rest after a long practice session. The two humans sat up and listened as hard as they could.

It sounded like the sea. But Raffa knew that they were too far from the Vast to hear the waves.

It could have been rain. A hard rain, steady and rhythmic. But although the night sky was cloudy, there was no smell of rain in the air.

Roo whined, then panted anxiously. Which she would not have done if she were hearing waves or rain.

Then Raffa knew what the sound was.

Boots.

The tread of thousands of guards' boots, marching through the fields but still a good distance away.

Kuma put a hand on his arm. "We have time," she said gently.

Only then did Raffa realize that he had jumped to his feet and was staring in the direction of the sound, his arms and legs and spine rigid. He blinked and nodded at Kuma, and took a long breath.

He turned to look in the other direction, back toward

the Forest. The moon struggled against the clouds, casting very little light on the landscape below. But if everything was going as planned, dozens of squads should now be arriving at the Mag from the Forest side. The Afters and their supporters would be positioning themselves behind the stone formations, hidden and waiting.

"We'll go on up now," Kuma said quietly.

Raffa offered a hand to pull her to her feet. She gave him a quick hug. "Ever Afters," she said with a smile.

"Ever Afters," he repeated.

It's true, he thought. *Kuma is full-After, and I'm half. Garith and Trixin and Jimble—none of them have After blood.* Somehow it felt right that he and Kuma were facing the first wave of the battle together, on their own.

He watched as Kuma and Roo and the raccoons walked up the slope of the Bridge. She turned to wave at him; he waved in return. Then he began hiking back in the direction of the Forest.

The sound of the approaching troops grew louder. The guards had nearly reached the Mag.

From a distance, Raffa heard Kuma's voice. "Freeze, Roo!"

He spun around just as the moon shoved aside the clouds, so he could see the Bridge clearly. Roo was curled up atop the highest point of the plateau. He couldn't see the raccoons; they were blocked by Roo's body. Against the dark sky, the bear looked like one of the many stone formations all over the Mag. If he hadn't known what to look for, he never would have spotted her.

As Raffa watched, Kuma left the animals on the plateau and dropped down out of sight. Assured that they were ready, he started moving faster. His aim was a nameless mass of stone at a point about a third of the way to the Forest. He had chosen it for two reasons: It put plenty of distance between him and the guards while still giving him a clear line of sight to what Kuma had called "a new stone formation—the Petrified Bear."

He reached the pile and climbed to its halfway point, where it narrowed perilously. For a moment he thought of securing himself with his leather rope—and then remembered that he no longer had it.

He stood on a narrow jut of stone, his weight forward so he was leaning against the bulk of the formation. The sound of the boots was slowly growing stronger; he kept staring out toward the edge of the Mag, but could see no movement.

Then the sound stopped. Abruptly and completely.

The guards had reached the Mag.

CHAPTER TWENTY-FIVE

RAFFA tried to imagine the guards' reactions at that moment. Most of them were Gildeners, unfamiliar with the Mag and the Forest. Even in full sunlight, the Mag was a mysterious place. But now, beneath the shifting light of an uncertain moon, the formations seemed otherworldly, as if they were monstrous creatures rather than solid stone. . . .

The guards would not be able to march rank-and-file through the lava field. The council had guessed that they would try to cross the Mag in patrols or platoons, and regroup on the far side, where there was a stretch of scrubland bordering the Forest.

After a few moments, Raffa heard the sound of boots again, but this time there was no regularity to it. And in the next interval of cloudless moon, he saw movement— what looked almost like water spilling into the Mag, narrowing into streams or spreading into puddles.

He waited, holding his breath. Some of the guards were now approaching the plateau.

Not long now . . . Come on, Roo, you can do it. . . .

He looked at the Bridge, where he could see the rounded mass at its highest point. In the next moment, clouds blocked the moon again and everything grew dim.

Now! Now, Kuma!

The mass began to move. Roo uncurled from her crouch and rose to her full height. Bando and Twig clung to her neck and shoulders, making her silhouette against the sky completely unrecognizable. A monster, an ogre, a horror from a nightmare . . . The raccoons were whipping their tails, swinging and swishing them; it looked like serpents were emerging from the monster's head.

Kuma's timing was perfect: Although Raffa could not hear her voice, he knew that she had given Roo the command.

The great golden bear threw back her head—and ROARED!

The sound was unbelievable. An earthquake. Thunder. A vortex from the bottom of the Vast, a bellow from the earth's very core. Even though he could barely see Roo, Raffa could feel her voice reverberating all around him.

In the midst of his awe, he smiled inwardly—at the image of Twig nonchalant and Bando with his eyes tightly closed.

The roar went on, and on, and on.

Finally Roo paused to draw a breath. At the same time, the moon emerged again; Raffa had the wild thought that it had been cowering behind the clouds, fearful of the bear's roar. Now it shone on a scene of chaos around the plateau.

Guards were fleeing in utter panic. Shrieks and screams cut through the air. Roo began to roar again, drowning out all other sound, but Raffa could still see the swarm of terror, everyone scrambling away from the Bridge, people running into each other, tripping, falling, dragging or knocking others down with them.

The second roar went on nearly as long as the first, and Raffa started to feel anxious.

That's enough, Kuma! Get away now—get out of there, all of you!

Their aim had been to frighten away as many guards as possible while not putting Roo or the raccoons in danger of being assailed by weaponry. Neither Raffa nor Kuma thought that the guards would be brave enough to approach Roo with a bluggen or lancer, but it was possible that the Chancellor had included archers among the troops. The animals had to get off the Bridge before any of the guards regained their nerve.

To his relief, he saw Roo drop to all fours and trundle down the stone ramp. She then disappeared from view, rejoining Kuma.

One final roar, the loudest and longest and the most frightening of all: The overwhelming sound appeared to be coming from the Mag itself. It seemed entirely possible that the whole lava field might explode from the pressure of the sound, spewing boulders into the air that would then come crashing down on anyone in their path.

Guards were still running away, dozens of them, maybe even hundreds, back toward the fields and farmsteads. Raffa allowed himself a brief satisfied vision of guards racing all the way to the river and plunging right into it, in their efforts to get away from the terrifying beast of stone.

* * *

Raffa climbed down from his perch. While Kuma was taking the animals back to the safety of the Forest, he was to join the Afters hiding deeper within the Mag.

Roo had frightened away many of the guards, but there were hundreds more continuing to advance. Raffa donned his mask to keep the blue glow from giving away his position, then set off. Being on his own and having some familiarity with the Mag meant that he could move faster than the guards. Still, his legs quickly grew tired: It was exhausting, having to put his foot down tentatively every single step, worried that the ground would be uneven or unstable or both.

When Raffa judged he was finally far enough ahead, he pushed the mask up on top of his head. Garith's idea for the blue-goo was having its first successful outing: The Afters would see the glow and know he was one of them.

"Hoy, young Santana!"

The relief of hearing Fitzer's voice gave Raffa new strength. He hurried over the last stretch of stony ground and soon saw Fitzer near the top of the formation known as the Angry Ox.

"I didn't know it would be you," Raffa said, panting. "I thought it was supposed to be Quellin's—I mean, Lantern Squad."

"Swapped with them," Fitzer said. "Made sense, since we're going to be with you later."

"Everyone else is here?"

Fitzer nodded. "Four squads altogether. There's a spot for you yonder," he said, and pointed behind them, in the direction of the Forest.

"But I—"

"Not having it," Fitzer said, cutting him off calmly but firmly. "Being at the front for your pothering tactic, that's one thing. But this is another, and you heard the council—no one under sixteen is even supposed to be out here. Don't make me regret letting you stay."

Raffa decided it would be unwise to protest further. He headed to the spot Fitzer had indicated. Along the way, he passed other Frypans. They were all wearing their masks, which reminded him to pull his down again. It was disconcerting to see the blank masks with their unnatural rectangular eye slits; he was glad when some folks nodded at him reassuringly.

He slipped behind yet another stone formation and readied himself, first by taking a deep draft from his waterskin. Then he pulled a willow whistle from his pocket.

Two dozen whistles had been distributed among the

squads; there hadn't been time to make more. Based on what he had heard and seen at the riverbank, Raffa's best guess was that the whistles were being used to guide or direct the animals in some way, with voice commands to order an attack. The squad members had been instructed to wait until they heard the guards' whistles, and to begin blowing their own in the hopes of confusing the animals, getting them to run every which way.

Raffa pushed up his mask just enough to clear his mouth; his glowing cheeks and forehead were still covered. Peering around the edge of his rock, he saw a few other Frypans hiding behind their own rocks. But his position wasn't elevated enough for him to see much of the landscape.

Again he waited.

I wonder if battles are always like this, so much waiting around. He had never known before that it was possible to be bored and scared at the same time.

But he didn't have long to wait. A hand opened and shut, outspread fingers and then a fist, the gesture passed along from After to After: the signal from Fitzer that the guards and animals were approaching.

* * *

Raffa's heart jumped. The time for him to make his stand was drawing nearer: He was to face the animals on his own in the scrubland between the Forest and the Mag. He leaned out cautiously from behind the rock.

A wild cacophony of whistles filled the air!

The Afters were all blowing on their whistles hard and fast. The noise was so shrill and constant that it was surely drowning out any attempts by the guards to issue whistled commands themselves. Raffa blew into his whistle again and again—long blasts and short toots, stopping only when he needed to replenish his breath.

Dizzy from the constant inhaling and exhaling, he saw the Frypans in front of him seem to hesitate—turning and looking back over their shoulders.

Someone shouted. Raffa couldn't make out the words.

The Frypans all began to run, stumbling on the treacherous basalt.

Something's wrong—why are they running this way?

One woman had taken off her mask; he could see her mouth moving, but he couldn't hear the words. There were too many people still whistling.

Then he saw a man gesturing wildly, waving his arms toward the Forest. It was Fitzer; he was masked, but Raffa recognized his sturdy build. Raffa waited until Fitzer had nearly reached him.

"FALL BACK!" Fitzer shouted. "It didn't work—they're coming! EVERYONE, FALL BACK!"

Raffa dropped the whistle he was holding and began to run. The Frypans were coalescing around Fitzer, trying to stay together. Raffa stumbled and fell to his knees. Someone grabbed his arm and yanked him to his feet again.

They had to get still farther into the Mag, where more squads awaited them. The stolen whistles were supposed to have scattered the animals, slowing their progress. If the plan had worked, the guards would have had to halt in order to get the animals organized again, giving Fitzer's squad and the others plenty of time to rejoin the rest of the Afters. Not only that, but the Afters had planned to use the whistles throughout the entire battle, to bewilder the animals at every turn.

Why isn't it working? What's gone wrong?

CHAPTER TWENTY-SIX

R AFFA panted desperately as he struggled across the unforgiving terrain. Ahead, he saw a masked After silhouetted against the sky and recognized Quellin.

"Frypans, Trowels, Pillows, Hammers!" she shouted. "Get behind our position!"

Raffa had nearly reached a stretch of ground that was clearer than its surroundings. Known as the Furrow, it looked almost like a road or a broad path—several paces in width and slightly humped in the center. He was familiar with it as one of the quicker ways to reach the Forest from the middle of the Mag. Hidden from view by rock formations, the Furrow was easy to miss unless you knew the area well.

He was able to run faster once he stepped onto the Furrow. Amidst the Frypans and members of three other squads, Raffa raced along for a short distance, then veered and scrambled to find a hiding place among the stone structures. Heart pounding, limbs trembling, he settled himself behind a pyramid of rock.

On either side of the Furrow, the Afters were waiting. Quellin's Lantern Squad and several more were ready with their blowpipes. In the hands of most of the Afters, the pipes had an alarmingly short range. They had to position themselves as close to the Furrow as possible to give themselves a chance at hitting the guards with the thorns. During blowpipe practice, a few people had shown some natural ability; their thorns flew much farther, and truer to the target. They had been assigned to positions at the beginning of the Furrow, and would try to hit the first guards to approach.

Raffa forced himself to take three deep breaths before opening his rucksack and extracting a blowpipe, a locuster pod, and a pair of gloves. His hands were shaking after the effort of his run; as he loaded his pipe, he dropped several thorns and cursed his clumsiness.

At last he was ready. A chain of murmurs made its way from After to After: "*Masks off. Pipes up.*"

An occasional flash caught Raffa's eye: The blue-goo was working beautifully. In the chaos that was sure to ensue, the Afters would be certain *not* to aim at anyone whose faces glowed blue.

There was, of course, the danger that the glow made them easier for the guards to spot. The council had come up with the idea that whenever possible, the squad members should raise and lower their masks at random intervals to confuse the guards.

Waiting.

Darkness.

The sound of boots on the Furrow's stone floor.

Then—"YOW! What's that?"

"Hoy! AH—it burns, it's burning!"

"YOW—my neck, my neck!"

The guards were being hit by touchrue thorns!

It's working, it's working!

But when Raffa dared a peek, he saw with dismay that dozens of guards were still advancing along the Furrow. Few of them seemed to have been afflicted by the thorns—a mere handful, who had stumbled off to the side.

We have to hit more of them!

Then he heard Fitzer call out, "Frypans! Hold your fire!"

The first phalanx of guards had nearly reached Raffa. What he saw next stunned him.

Fitzer ran out into the Furrow directly in front of the guards. As he dashed to the other side, he blew a continuous stream of thorns at the guards.

Almost every one of his thorns hit a guard! Nearly the entire first row broke ranks while they clapped their hands to their necks or their faces, crying out in agony.

"Frypans!" Fitzer shouted. "Did you see that? Show and go, show and go! Stay out of bluggen range!"

The man nearest to Raffa stepped out from behind his cover, blue cheeks clearly visible. "I'm go!" he yelled, and crossed the Furrow just as Fitzer had, shooting thorns the whole way.

From the other side of the Furrow, the Pillows' leader hollered.

"I'm go!" she shouted. "Pans and Pillows, alternate!" Her thorns, too, hit their targets much more often at such close range.

From one side to the other, Afters crisscrossed the Furrow, sending a near constant stream of thorns at the guards. A good number of the guards were hit more than once; they were doubled over in pain from the combination of piercing thorn, touchrue sap, and nettle essence. So many of them had stopped that the forward progress of the column pounding down the Furrow had slowed to a near standstill.

Raffa quickly climbed the nearest formation for a better view. The darkness was just beginning to thin, and he was puzzled by what he saw: There seemed to be a considerable gap in the ranks of the guards.

Why would they have left a space like that?

He strained to see farther. The first shafts of daybirth sunlight reached along the Furrow at an oblique angle—and he gasped in horror.

The gap was not empty.

Dozens of pairs of gleaming purple eyes seemed to be staring straight at him.

The animals!

Raffa knew that the eyes of animals treated with the scarlet-vine infusion took on a purple sheen. He had noticed it in Echo, and Bando and Twig, and the animals trapped in the compound. But never before had he seen so many of the treated animals in one place.

For a moment that seemed removed from time, he

stared, mesmerized by the sight. The tiny purple lights—
how beautiful they were! They could have been stars, or
jewels, or sparks from a magical fire. . . .

Then one pair of the purple lights rose higher than
the others—and snapped Raffa out of his trance. It was
a fox or a stoat, leaping into the air.

"The animals!" he shouted. "Fitzer, we have to
move!"

Fitzer responded immediately. "FRYPANS! ALL
SQUADS, TO POSITION THREE!"

Along with the other Afters, Raffa once again began
the thankless task of trying to move quickly through the
Mag. He glanced over his shoulder. Were the guards still
delayed by the thorn attack? Could he risk running on
the Furrow instead?

The guards had advanced no farther. Raffa felt a
moment of exultation. "Fitzer!" he called. "They're not
moving—can we use the Furrow?"

Fitzer looked and saw what Raffa had seen. "Frypans, with me!" he hollered, and ran out onto the clearer
ground.

The other squads followed the Frypans, and soon a
dozen squads were racing down the middle of the Furrow. The guards were not pursuing them. If that were

the case, the Afters at the back would have passed on a warning—and would have been running with far more urgency.

Why aren't they chasing us? What are they waiting for?

To his right, the sun was now peering over the horizon. Raffa felt his spirits rise. The Afters had done their best to use the darkness to their advantage, but he had hated the uncertainty of not being able to see clearly.

"Hoy!" someone yelled.

Raffa turned his head to the left and saw a woman pointing to the west.

"Birds!" she shouted. "A lot of them!"

CHAPTER TWENTY-SEVEN

"CROWS!" Raffa screamed. "MASKS, EVERY-ONE! MASKS!"

He yanked his mask down as all around him other Afters did the same.

That was why the guards had stopped advancing! The crows were trained to attack anything that stood on two legs—meaning, mostly humans. But they wouldn't be able to tell the difference between one side and the other, so the guards were staying back after the crows had been released.

If the masks work . . . if the crows can't tell where our eyes are, and don't attack—this will be our chance to get out of the Mag well ahead of the guards.

He kept running, and kept looking to his left. The crows were drawing nearer.

Hundreds of them.

They flocked together like an enormous black cloud, ragged at the edges. The cloud seemed to suck every bit of light out of the sky and the air. There was no shine of glossy feathers, no flicker or flutter of wings, no cawing or calls. The crows moved as if they were a single, silent, ominous being.

The rim of the black cloud was now nearly overhead. Raffa looked up, his range of vision limited by the mask. The cloud seemed to hover for a moment, holding its breath.

Then the first crows dove.

They plummeted out of the sky as if they were sleek black arrows. With a twist to his gut that nearly made him sick, Raffa knew the awful truth: *The masks were not fooling them.*

The crows struck hard. The thin birchbark masks were no match for the birds' cruel beaks: A single strike tore a hole in the bark, which immediately began to shred, leaving the Afters' faces exposed.

"DOWN, EVERYONE!" Fitzer yelled. "COVER!"

Raffa spotted a stone formation with a ledge over-hang. He ran to his right and threw himself under the ledge. The overhang was good protection from the crows, none of which bothered to attack him. It was far easier for them to dive at those out on the open Furrow.

Horrified, he watched the crows' relentless attack. People were crouched on the ground with their arms over their heads. The crows struck wherever they could—heads, necks, arms, hands. Raffa heard the cries of pain and saw the birds draw blood again and again. The only sounds were coming from the humans. The crows were utterly, eerily silent.

The Afters had to get moving. *If the guards start to advance again—if they give the foxes and stoats the command to attack while we're like this—we won't have a chance.*

Somehow there had to be a way to beat off the crows. Too late Raffa realized that he had dropped his blow-pipe and cursed himself for it. *Maybe I could have hit them with thorns!*

He knew that the idea was impractical: It was one thing to hit the guards, large targets that were practi-cally standing still. The crows, in constant motion, would have been all but impossible to hit.

But it was the only thing he could think of. He looked around desperately, trying to spot Fitzer. With everyone curled up, he could not find him.

"FITZER!" he screamed. "FITZER, WHERE ARE YOU? THE PIPES—THE THORNS—WE HAVE TO—"

He was almost sobbing now at the horrific sight before him: the crows, the countless crows, diving and striking, diving and striking, so many that there was barely a breath in between. The Afters would never be able to escape, and soon—how soon?—the foxes and stoats and wolves would be upon them.

Then he heard an odd noise. For a brief moment he didn't know what he was hearing. The sound continued and grew louder, and he realized what it was.

The crows were squawking. All this time, they had been completely silent. Raffa frowned—what was making them squawk now?

He risked leaning out for a better look. Before him, the crows were squawking and flapping, rising up and away from their targets. They were clearly retreating. Completely baffled, Raffa glanced up at the sky.

No matter how long he lived, he would never forget what he saw there.

Bats.

Bats!

A wide, sweeping, endless ribbon of bats, just as he had last seen them at the gorge! Thousands upon thousands of them!

Only a moment earlier, the flock of crows had seemed like an infinite number of birds. Now they looked piddling and insignificant against the incredible mass of bats filling the sky above the Mag.

The bats were making what looked to Raffa like halfhearted attempts to engage the crows in a fight. But with a few hundred crows facing several thousand bats, there was no need. Intelligent birds, the crows appeared to realize instantly that they had no chance. They could not get away fast enough.

Raffa scooted out from under the ledge, then climbed on top of it. He wanted to see what the guards were doing.

In front of him, the Afters had uncurled from their crouches. Most had removed their masks. Much farther down the Furrow, the guards were seemingly frozen, their boots glued to the ground as if they had stepped in sticky puddles of irongum sap. Afters and guards alike, every single face was turned skyward, watching the endless stream of bats in awe and wonder.

The magnificent skein of bats was beginning to turn. Like the oxbow of a river, an enormous, graceful curve formed, the bats following an invisible undulating loop in the air. They had come from the south, from the gorge, and having quickly dispatched every last crow, they were swerving around to return home again.

As if by instinct, Raffa raised his arm, holding it out straight. He hadn't seen or heard anything different; somehow he just knew.

Whump.

"Ouch!"

The soft impact of a very small animal hitting his sleeve, followed by that beloved squeaky voice.

Raffa drew in his arm so that Echo, hanging upside down near his elbow, was right in front of his face.

"Well, hello there," he said as gently as his thrilled heart would allow. "Echo good?"

The bat chirped and chirred. "Raffa go, Echo come!"

Raffa stroked Echo behind the ears. He could hardly believe that the bat had returned; at the same time, being with him immediately felt familiar and comfortable. *I wonder . . . if that's what love is. When familiar things make you feel really good.*

But at the moment, he had more pressing things to think about. He knew that, with Echo's limited vocabulary, he would get very little explanation for the sudden and miraculous appearance of the bats. But he wanted to try anyway.

"Echo, why did you come? Did you know that I—I needed your help?"

"Birds many," Echo replied. "Birds many no good."

Raffa marveled at the bat's response. Echo had been there the first time Raffa had seen the trained crows attack humans.

"You remembered! But how did you know that the crows would be *here*? And how did you get all the other bats to come with you?"

Squeak squeak. "Birds many no good," Echo repeated.

Apparently, these questions were too much for the little bat. Or maybe, Raffa thought, there will always be things about animals that we'll never quite understand.

"Right," Raffa said. "It's not important. I'm so glad you're here."

During their brief conversation, both the Afters and the guards had begun to tear their attention away from the mesmerizing sight of the bats overhead. Now Raffa saw Fitzer jump to his feet and toss away his torn mask.

"EARS, FRYPANS!" Fitzer shouted. "POSITION FOUR!"

His squad obeyed instantly, amid a flurry of identical orders from the other leaders to their squads. The sun was fully risen now, and in its light, Raffa was horrified to see that many of the Afters' faces were bloodied from the injuries that the crows had inflicted before being dispersed by the bats. He cursed himself.

We could have made a healing salve and given everyone a little jar—why didn't I think of that?

He took some comfort from the fact that none of the wounds appeared to be life-threatening, and soon the Furrow was once again filled with Afters jog-trotting to their next destination.

Raffa turned to the little bat on his arm and spoke quickly. "Echo, you—you probably want to go back with the other bats. But would you . . . could you stay with me for a little while? And I'll take you back to the gorge myself, as soon as I can."

The battle would not last longer than the morning, he was sure of it. Either the Afters would prevail or . . .

Or people would die.

Maybe a lot of people. Including those he cared

about—people he loved.

He desperately wanted Echo's company, and the bat might well be useful in the fight. But he would not keep Echo here against his will. He held his breath, waiting for the answer.

Echo's wings twitched a little.

"Perch?" he said.

Overjoyed, Raffa pulled the perch necklace out of his rucksack and put it on. Echo took his place on the twig, hanging below the knitted collars that Raffa was wearing around his neck.

"Hang on tight, Echo," Raffa said.

Then he raced to catch up with the Frypans.

CHAPTER TWENTY-EIGHT

THE Furrow rose on a slight angle, then flattened out again as it reached the stretch of scrubland marking the border between the Mag and the Forest. The Afters, their blue cheeks still glowing, began arranging themselves by squad in staggered rows that filled the whole area, with more Afters positioned within the Forest itself. Each After stood centered in a wide circle of space, at least two arm's lengths away from anyone else.

Plenty of space . . . for an animal to jump.

At the front edge of the scrub, Raffa spoke to Fitzer.

"I'll be my own row, at the front," he said, his mouth dry. He rushed on before Fitzer could protest. "At the meeting I said that I would stand alone, and I—I can't go back on my word."

Fitzer frowned. "You're giving me a bit of a problem," he said. "See, I'd not stand in the way of anyone honest trying to keep their word. But I gave *my* word, too. To your mam and da. Promised them I'd look after you."

Raffa stared at him, caught between irritation and affection. *Do they think I can't take care of myself?* Still, it was clear that his parents had been thinking of him. And he spared a thought for them now, realizing that their worry about him must be squeezing their hearts nearly every moment.

"You wouldn't be breaking your word," he said. "You'll be there, if—if anything happens."

Fitzer began to speak, but Raffa held up his hand. "I'm talking logic," he said. "If this works, I'll be fine. I have enough antidote for at least half a dozen animals, and I doubt that many will attack me. And if it doesn't work, I—I'll surrender right away. So there's no need for anyone else to—to risk getting hurt."

He looked at Fitzer's face steadily, including in his gaze the livid birthmark with its scars and pitting. Raffa saw those things and knew they had nothing to do with the man's mind and heart.

No. That's not right. He's the way he is at least partly because of how he looks. His face . . . people have been unkind to him.

Raffa had seen for himself how some people in the camp had recoiled from Fitzer's appearance. Fitzer could have returned such unkindness at every opportunity, but he chose to do the opposite. Raffa wondered how hard it would be to do that; Fitzer made it seem easy.

Maybe kindness can get to be a habit for a person. Like a lot of other things.

"Please, Mannum Fitzer," Raffa said quietly. "I have to do this."

"Right," Fitzer said, "I'll stand behind you, then."

Raffa nodded. Saying "thank you" hardly seemed adequate. But what else was there to say?

"Thank you," he said. Then he turned and began jogging straight toward the source of his fear.

Raffa counted his steps. He wanted to put a good distance between himself and the other Afters. If things did not go as planned, he would surrender immediately, and hope that the guards would call off the attack before the animals reached the Frypans.

After some thirty paces, he stopped and looked around. He was standing at a spot where the Mag petered out into scrubland. Because of the slight rise near the end of the Furrow, he would not see the guards until they were nearly upon him. But he would be able to hear them.

Reluctantly, he took from his rucksack the stick he had prepared, with a long white strip of cloth tied to the end. The traditional streamer of surrender, which he would wave overhead in a large figure-eight motion . . .

If the antidote tactic didn't work.

If he had to surrender.

If he was still on his feet and able to wave it.

He was as ready as he could be. Two knitted sacks filled with antidote powder tied around each ankle. A piece of leather circling his neck, with two collars on top of it. The streamer stick tucked into his belt, at the back.

He took the perch necklace out from underneath his tunic and spoke briefly to Echo.

"Echo, will you wait for me in those trees over there?" He waved toward the Forest. He was taking no chances that the bat would be injured either by animal or human. "I'll whistle for you, okay?"

"Echo go, Raffa come," the bat said, and flew off.

Raffa listened hard. It wasn't long before he heard the steady thump of guards' boots on the Furrow. The animals among them made no sound, which was some-how more frightening than if he had been able to hear them.

He heard something else, too: whistles.

The whistles were being blown *in patterns.*

High-high-low. High-low-high. Low-high-low.

That was why the whistle tactic hadn't worked! The animals had been trained to respond not to random whistle blasts but to specific patterns of tones. His mind flashed back to the night on the bank of the Everwide, where he had first learned that the guards were using whistles to command the animals.

I was in a hurry to get to a boat, to get across. And everything was confusing. I heard the sound of whistles being blown. . . . That was all. . . .

But the whistled patterns now sounded familiar, and he realized that he had indeed heard them that night. Heard them, and then not taken them into account.

Raffa groaned, angry at himself once again. *I didn't think about it enough. I just thought "whistles," and made up the plan and never thought about it after that. It's my fault that it didn't work.*

It was not the first time he had failed to think things through, failed to consider that there might be other angles and wrinkles to what he thought was a good idea.

And I never really talked about it to anyone else, either.

HIGH-HIGH-LOW

HIGH-HIGH-LOW

The whistle blasts were much closer now. His head jerked, and his heart began thumping so hard that he thought his chest might burst. The guards were cresting the slight rise, and the first of them came into view.

Those at the front of the column began peeling off to the sides as they reached the end of the Furrow. Seeing this, Raffa knew that he and the council had guessed correctly: The guards were sending the animals to attack first.

Now, at last, he heard the lighter footfalls of the animals, which he would not have been able to detect if there hadn't been so many of them.

Dozens.

Hundreds.

And a moment later, he was staring at row upon row of beautiful, eerie purple eyes.

The gleams of purple nearest him were low to the ground, part of a mass of lithe, sinuous bodies.

"Stoats," he whispered.

He remembered seeing their vicious attack at Kuma's settlement: In what seemed a mere blink of time, a pack of stoats had killed dozens of chickens, each bird the victim of a single lethal bite to the head.

LOW-HIGH-LOW

LOW-HIGH-LOW

Then a voice rang out clearly. "SHARP, SNAP!"

A stoat separated itself from the pack. How small it looked on its own! Barely the length and girth of a toddler's forearm . . . but Raffa knew that its size belied its fierceness. The image of its sharp teeth snapping hard into his throat—he thought for a moment that he might faint.

The stoat jumped in the air, writhing and twisting as it landed. It sprang forward and jumped again, then began racing toward Raffa.

Raffa wanted to run so badly that his feet began to itch. He was sweating, and at the same time shaking so hard that his teeth were chattering. *What if the sacks don't burst? What if the antidote doesn't work? What if a whole pack attacks me at once?*

Fear made his vision blur and his ears pound; a bitter taste of metal filled his mouth. *What if I didn't think this through, either—if I made some kind of mistake, like with the whistles?*

Then a series of images swirled through his mind in rapid succession. Faces, mostly.

Da, teaching him how to boil a residue.

Mam, showing him how to knit so he could make his own tunic, the very one he wore now.

And most of all, Garith.

Everything about the antidote powder and the knitted sacks had been discussed with Garith. They had made the combination together. Raffa had thought of the collars. Garith had proposed tying them off in sections. They had turned the problem inside out, upside down, back-to-front, arguing, questioning, discussing.

It wasn't just me by myself. It was other people, too, especially Garith.

This will work—I know it will.

A sudden stillness fell over him as he watched the stoat get closer and closer. His sweats and tremors seemed almost chilled by a strange sense of calm and coolness.

He planted his feet firmly, then turned his head one way and his shoulder the other, exposing as much of the side of his neck as he possibly could.

The stoat jumped, and struck.

CHAPTER TWENTY-NINE

A<small>T</small> the last moment, Raffa closed his eyes and held his breath. With an angry hiss, the stoat sank its teeth into the knitted collar.

Powder burst from the tear in the fabric and clouded the air—while Raffa's neck was completely untouched!

But the stoat's mouth was clamped firmly on the collar, and the animal was still hanging on. With a cry of alarm, Raffa shook himself hard, and the stoat dropped to the ground.

Raffa backed away from the creature, while keeping his eyes on it every second. The stoat seemed dazed for a moment. It sneezed, and pawed at its nose.

Then it straightened up and looked around, sniffing the air.

It dashed away—not back to the guards, nor toward the Afters, but to the west, where it would soon find the meadows that were its natural home.

Raffa allowed himself a single breath of relief. As another series of whistle blasts filled the air, he turned and ran, with a whole slew of stoats and foxes on his heels.

"IT WORKED!" he shouted to Fitzer. "THEY'RE COMING!"

"Stand your ground, Frypans!" Fitzer called out. "Necks, full exposure!"

Raffa found a spot between two Frypans. Quickly he adjusted the collars around his neck so the emptied section was at the back. Then he took up his stance again.

This time, a fox ran at him, bigger and heavier than the stoat. And more frightening: Raffa had thought that getting through the first attack would give him some confidence. But seeing the fox's sharp teeth exposed in a slavering grin, he felt fear flooding through him even more strongly than before.

The fox leapt at him so hard that he was knocked off his feet. He landed almost flat on his back, with the fox on his neck, growling in his ear, its hot breath heavy with fox-stink. Antidote powder fell like snow on both him and the fox. It was standing on his chest now, about to snap its jaws again—

Raffa shrieked in terror. He was groping blindly at his neck when the fox, like the stoat before it, suddenly sneezed once, twice. It blinked and shook its head from side to side. Then it jumped off his chest and ran west.

Panting, Raffa lay back in exhaustion. Voices filled the air. Some people roared or bellowed to hearten themselves and their companions; triumphant yells were mixed with cries of fear.

He struggled to his feet. When his vision cleared, he couldn't help a wordless shout at what he saw: All around him, animals were fleeing westward.

We did it, we did it! Where was Garith? And Kuma? Were they seeing this, the animals returned to their natural state, running away to avoid contact with humans? *It's happening just like we thought it would!*

Then Raffa heard a scream.

"HELP! SOMEONE, PLEASE—HELP—HELP!"

It was Jimble.

* * *

Raffa ran toward the sound of Jimble's voice. He had to weave his way through the chaos of what was surely the strangest battle ever waged: stoats and foxes and badgers against humans, most of whom were not fighting back: They were standing as still as statues while the animals attacked.

But there was still a tumult of motion, as people kept running to put themselves in the way of another creature.

Motion—and noise.

Shouts of panic.

Cries of fear.

Screams of pain.

As Raffa ran, images blurred in his vision, a nightmare echo of what he had seen during the river crossing. A man tripping and falling as a badger savaged his ankle. A fox with its teeth clamped on a woman's forearm. Another man with a stoat clinging to his neck, blood streaming . . .

The Afters were prevailing. The number of animals fleeing far outnumbered those that were on the attack. Guards were screaming orders and blowing whistles; the animals that had inhaled the powder ignored them completely.

But still, people were getting hurt—some of them badly. For a long, agonized moment, Raffa couldn't decide what to do—keep trying to find Jimble? Or stop and help the injured here?

He was nearing the Forest when he heard Jimble scream again, very nearby. The voice of a friend who needed help was something Raffa could not ignore. He whirled around, searching, searching—

"RAFFA! HELP ME!"

Jimble was cornered. He had backed into a copse formed by touchrue shrubs on three sides; he could not move in any direction except forward.

In front of the copse, pacing back and forth, was an enormous wolf.

Then the huge creature lowered itself to its belly. It was no longer stalking Jimble. It was preparing to attack.

Raffa didn't think; there was no time to think. He simply reacted.

He yanked the knitted sack off his left wrist. Bellowing at the top of his lungs, he raced straight toward the wolf.

He was too late. The wolf sprang, aiming for one of its prey's extremities: Jimble's leg.

Jimble screamed as the wolf's jaws closed around his calf.

In blind fear and fury, Raffa leapt forward and hit the wolf on the nose with the sack as hard as he could. The sack burst with an explosion of powder. The wolf yelped and released its grip on Jimble's leg. It shook its head in confusion, snorting and pawing at its nose.

"Climb on my back!" Raffa said to Jimble, whose eyes were glazing over in shock and pain. "Jimble, NOW!"

Jimble managed to fling himself onto Raffa's back. The wolf raised its nose in the air and howled.

"GET AWAY!" Raffa shouted, and threw the sack at the wolf.

The antidote had taken effect. The wolf yelped, backed up, and then turned and loped away.

Raffa staggered into the Forest. He had to get Jimble somewhere safe.

"Raffa! What happened?" Garith came running toward him. "He was here with me, and then the animals— He ran ahead of me and I couldn't find him—" He took a now-unconscious Jimble off Raffa's back.

"Wolf," Raffa said, barely able to get the words out. "His leg." He pointed, but there was no need. Blood still streamed from the wound.

"I've got him," Garith said, hoisting Jimble's limp body in his arms. He looked at Raffa over the top of Jimble's blond head. "I'll take care of him. You get back to the fight."

Raffa cast a last worried glance at Jimble, then looked at his cousin. "Take care of yourself, too," he said.

Wolves.

It wasn't that he had forgotten about them. It was more that he hadn't thought much about them in the first place. He had witnessed the stoats and the foxes in action before, and he'd seen the badgers in the secret compound. But he'd never actually laid eyes on the wolves.

And then he hadn't wanted to think about them, and there had been so many other things on his mind. . . .

Well, *I'm thinking about them now,* he thought grimly.

At the secret compound, he had seen two locked sheds set apart from the rest, and according to Echo, each shed had held two wolves. Four altogether. That in itself was remarkable, as wolves were rare in Obsidia. Raffa thought it highly unlikely that Jayney and Trubb, the Chancellor's men, had been able to find any more.

Three left, then.

Raffa had been trotting back toward the battle. He stopped to get himself organized. He took the knitted sacks from his neck and ankles, as well as the strip of leather, and transferred everything to his left forearm. The collars wrapped twice around his arm, each making a double layer. Now his arm was well protected, but at the expense of the entire rest of his body.

He knew that wolves hunted by singling out the most vulnerable prey, and that, as had happened to Jimble, they often targeted extremities—legs and, for humans, arms, too. He would be using both of those pieces of knowledge.

"Raffa!"

It was Fitzer. Raffa quickly explained about the wolves and what he was planning. "I have to track them down," he said. "I saw how that one wolf attacked. No one else knows what to expect."

Fitzer immediately moved all his sacks to one forearm, just as Raffa had done.

"Let's go," he said.

They made their way to the east side of the scrub-land, away from the most frenzied activity. Putting several paces between them, they both began affecting limps, moving slowly and hesitantly.

It did not take long before Raffa heard a far-off whistle, then spotted a pair of purple eyes coming toward him—on an animal far larger than a fox.

Behind it, two more pairs of eyes.

All three wolves.

They were hunting in a pack.

"Raffa," Fitzer said, his voice calm but urgent. "Back-to-back."

Keeping his eyes on the wolves, Raffa edged his way toward Fitzer until they were standing back-to-back. The wolves drew nearer and began pacing in a semicircle, but made no move to attack.

"It's you they want," Fitzer said.

Raffa swallowed. "I know." *They always choose the smaller one. Or the weaker.* "They're not going to try as long as you're so close. I'm going to step away again."

"Watch yourself, lad."

Raffa put several paces between himself and Fitzer. The three wolves were grouped together, all clearly focused on him. The largest one was enormous, and had a great ruff around its neck. It separated itself from the others and began moving toward him, slowly but purposefully.

For a long moment, everything seemed frozen in time.

The wolf charged.

CHAPTER THIRTY

RAFFA thrust out his left arm. As the wolf sprang, he could see nothing but its mouth, wide open, with enormous jagged teeth. Unable to bear the terrifying sight, he squeezed his eyes shut.

The wolf struck his arm so hard that he spun around from the force of the blow. With its teeth gripping the knitted fabric of the sacks, the wolf shook its head, hard. It tugged and pulled, snapping its jaws repeatedly. A choking haze of antidote powder filled the air. Raffa heard the wolf snort, and felt it release his arm.

But to his horror, the wolf did not flee, as the other treated animals had. It bounded a few paces away, then circled around and was now staring at him again, its tongue out, panting and drooling.

Raffa took a quick glance down at his arm. He was uninjured, but only one of the knitted sacks was still intact; the others had been shredded by the wolf's vicious teeth. He guessed then that the antidote was taking longer to work because the wolf was so large.

Panic made him want to run. He took a step back, his gaze on the big wolf. Then he sensed movement to his left.

"Don't look at me," Fitzer said quietly. "Stay right where you are. Keep its attention on you, if you can."

The calm in Fitzer's voice steadied Raffa. Holding his breath, he stared into the wolf's eyes. *Look at me look at me look at me. . . .*

Fitzer dove in front of him. The wolf reached Raffa at the same moment, knocking him to the ground. Fitzer and Raffa and the wolf were all tangled up, arms and legs, tail and snout, the wolf growling, Fitzer grunting, Raffa gasping, the breath slapped from his lungs.

The wolf's growl changed to a whine. Then Raffa saw that one of its front paws was snarled in the knitted sacks wrapped around Fitzer's forearm. As Fitzer started to stand up, the wolf tried to flee. It jerked so hard that

Fitzer was yanked off his feet and fell forward. The knitted sacks stretched out: Fitzer bellowed a curse as his arm was twisted and wrenched. Raffa heard a sickening *pop* from Fitzer's shoulder.

Finally the big wolf managed to free itself and ran away.

"All right?" Raffa asked.

"Not a scratch," Fitzer said but with a grimace, and Raffa knew that he must be in terrible pain.

There was no time for worrying over it now. Raffa jumped to his feet to see the last two wolves pacing uncertainly, turning their heads back and forth to look from Raffa to the west, where their companion had disappeared.

No no no—not yet, you two, don't you dare leave yet—

He had to stop them from fleeing! If they weren't dosed with the antidote, they might attack someone else, or end up sick or dying in the wild.

He took his one remaining sack in hand. "Stay down," he hissed at Fitzer.

He began moving slowly toward the wolves, keeping low to the ground, using a hobbled, hesitant gait. He was trying to appear as vulnerable as he could.

Look, wolves. See how small I am? You could—you could eat me for breakfast.

He couldn't help shuddering. If these two attack me the way the big one did, I'm a dead dog, Raffa thought. *Dead dead dead—*

And then he knew what to do.

"*Stay down,*" he repeated to Fitzer.

He limped a few paces closer to the wolves. Then he began making crying, whining noises, as if he were in pain. When he was certain of their interest, he fell to the ground, turning to land on his back with his hands on his chest.

He lay as still as he could, except for his fingers. They were working furiously, untying the end of the sack he held.

The wolves approached slowly. Raffa kept his eyes half-closed, watching them without meeting their gazes. For this to work, he would need them to be almost on top of him.

Come on, he begged silently. *Closer, closer . . .*

The next few moments seemed to last years. Would the wolves ever get near enough? Raffa strained against himself: If he moved too soon, it might not work—and he wouldn't get a second chance.

NOT YET NOT YET NOT YET, he screamed inside his head.

Finally the wolves were only a step away. Raffa sat up and threw the sack right at them. Untied, the sack sprayed its powder as it flew through the air, while Raffa immediately curled back up into a small tight ball.

One wolf growled, long and low. Raffa had never known that a quiet noise could be so frightening. Head in his arms, he could not see what the wolves were doing.

The growl ended abruptly—in a sneeze.

The wolf sneezed and sneezed and sneezed. Raffa uncurled just enough to take a peek. He saw the wolf pawing at its nose. It whimpered, then put its face in the dirt, rubbing vigorously. Finally it threw back its head and shook it hard before trotting off to the west.

The other wolf yipped twice. Raffa turned to look at it, and knew at once that it had not inhaled any of the antidote. It hadn't sneezed or pawed its nose, and more than that, it lacked the almost indefinable quality of the animals that had been treated: Simply put, they acted wild again.

Raffa tensed. He was now defenseless, having used up the last of the sacks.

"Do you have any sacks left?" he asked Fitzer, keeping his voice low.

"They're all torn," Fitzer answered, "but there's some powder left in them—"

The last wolf let out a long howl, followed by a series of yips. Then it began running toward the west.

Raffa leapt to his feet. "No!" he cried out. He started chasing after the wolf, but had taken only a few paces when he realized that he would never be able to catch it.

He watched until he couldn't see it any longer, his heart pounding. Tears filled his eyes at the vision of what the untreated wolf would face over the next day or so: twitching, shivering, fever, pain, vomiting. . . . There was only a slim chance that it would survive the terrible symptoms of withdrawal from its addiction to the scarlet-vine infusion.

He knew, too, that there were surely other untreated animals: It was too much to hope that every single creature had inhaled the powder. Heartsick, he let loose a curse of frustration and anger at the Chancellor. Wasn't there enough suffering in the world for both humans and animals, without deliberately causing more?

* * *

"We have to hurry," Fitzer said as he got to his feet. "The clearing."

As they began to run, Raffa saw that Fitzer was holding his left arm against his side. Raffa had watched his parents treat wrenched shoulders, although he had never done it himself.

"Your arm," Raffa said. "I might be able to—"

Fitzer shook his head. "No time. I'll be okay."

They kept running. When they reached the edge of the Forest, Raffa whistled for Echo. He was relieved to hear the whirring of the bat's wings almost immediately. Echo landed on Raffa's shoulder with his usual "Ouch!"

Raffa picked Echo up and stroked him for a moment. "Echo, listen. I need you to fly toward the river, and see if anyone is coming this way. On horses."

"Horse come."

"Yes. My mam—remember her? It might be her, and she'll be with someone else, at least I hope she will. I know it's your time to sleep, so you don't have to search for very long, okay? Then come back and find me."

"Mam horse."

"And don't forget—stay away from any other people."

Raffa gave the little bat a last scratch before releasing him and watching him fly away.

* * *

Fitzer had gone ahead. Raffa tried to resume running, but he felt like he was wading through irongum sap, his legs leaden with exhaustion. The best he could manage was to trot, trying not to fall too far behind.

He tallied things in his head. It was clear that the guards had saved the wolves for last. By now the squads should have been able to disperse the other animals. Roo had frightened off a good many guards, so there would be fewer of them in pursuit of the Afters. The touchrue thorns had delayed still more guards, and it would take time for them to reach the clearing.

Have we done enough? Has Mam been able to bring the Advocate back to himself? If he's not on his way here, all of this will have been for nothing.

No. Not for nothing. They had managed to treat hundreds of animals and free them from their captors.

That's something. Better than something. For the animals, but also because it shows the Chancellor that we can beat her. Even if we don't defeat her today, we showed her that she can't have her way with everything.

The path was deserted, which made the going easier. Raffa caught up with Fitzer. As they drew nearer to the clearing, Raffa frowned.

It was too quiet. He should have been able to hear something. Voices, at least. He was about to say something when Fitzer spoke.

"Too quiet," Fitzer said, and slowed his pace.

Raffa thought aloud. "All the squads should have reached the clearing by now," he said. "It would be easy for them—they know the way. And the guards followed them. And we were delayed because of the wolves, so . . . everyone is there except us?"

"That would be my guess, too," Fitzer said. "Just seems strange that it's so quiet."

The squads' orders had been to retreat to the clearing. They were not to wage battle against the guards: Even with the guards' numbers reduced, it would be a slaughter. Their objective was to delay the guards as long as possible, in the hope that the Advocate would reach the clearing and rescind the Chancellor's orders.

The guards would be trying to remove the Afters from the clearing—either to force them to leave Obsidia or to arrest them. The squads were to be as uncooperative as possible without provoking violence.

"Sit on the ground with your hands in plain sight," Quellin had advised the squad leaders. "You can even lie down."

"If they pick you up, go completely limp," Elson had added. "Don't struggle, but be a deadweight—make it hard for them to move you."

"Absolutely no striking out," Haddie had said. "It will take only one mistake for them to retaliate against all of us."

Raffa and Fitzer were approaching the stable area of the camp. Fitzer held up his hand for quiet. They edged up to a large locuster tree. Fitzer was peering around it cautiously when Raffa felt something poking his side. Momentarily confused, he wondered if he had leaned against something sharp. Then—

"GOT HIM!"

Raffa turned to see Jayney holding a javelancer, the tip of which was prodding his side. On Jayney's face was an expression of cruel triumph. Four armed guards flanked him.

"Move," Jayney said, jerking his head and his lancer toward the clearing.

Both Raffa and Fitzer immediately sat down on the ground.

"Quake's sake! Not again," muttered one of the other guards.

A brief moment of satisfaction: Clearly, the other

Afters had followed their squad leaders' orders.

The guards wasted no time. On Jayney's orders, Raffa's and Fitzer's hands were bound with rope. Then one guard lifted Raffa under his arms and another grabbed his feet. Two more guards did the same to Fitzer; Raffa heard him stifle a cry of pain.

They were half-dragged, half-carried along the path into the clearing. Raffa saw row after row of Afters sitting on the ground, with their hands behind their heads. Guards stood among them, weapons threatening.

As he and Fitzer were dumped near the pavilion, Raffa heard a voice he knew too well.

"Young Santana! I'm so pleased to see you again."

It was the Chancellor. She stood on the dais at the front of the pavilion, her silver hair gleaming like a helmet.

At her side was Uncle Ansel.

CHAPTER THIRTY-ONE

RAFFA refused to meet his uncle's gaze. He turned his head away to search the pavilion. Where was Garith? And Jimble, and Kuma? Was Jimble all right?

Most pressing of all, *Where was the Advocate?*

A cadre of guards was marching toward the pavilion.

"Mannum Trubb," the Chancellor called, "please escort young Santana to the dais. I would like him to welcome our guests with me."

Raffa was always amazed at how normal the Chancellor sounded when she spoke. He thought grimly that it would be much easier to tell who the enemy was if they would at least look or sound evil. *But they don't. They look and sound like anyone else.*

Trubb stepped down from the dais. Raffa remembered seeing him in Gilden months earlier: a tall, pale, stringy man who worked for Senior Jayney.

"On your feet," Trubb said, his voice high-pitched and snivelly, as if he had a perpetual cold. He prodded Raffa's leg with his toe.

Raffa didn't move.

"I said, on your feet!" Trubb screeched.

"Never mind," the Chancellor said. "I believe young Santana will join us of his own accord."

With a sweep of her arm, she indicated the group of guards who had nearly reached the dais. Now Raffa could see that the guards were clustered around two people who wore hooded cloaks. Their hands were tied in front of them.

Prisoners, Raffa thought, and he shivered from a sudden chill.

As the guards moved aside, the Chancellor stepped down from the dais. She herself pulled back the hood of one prisoner and then the other.

Raffa's mother, Salima, was one of the prisoners. The other was Trixin.

Raffa was on his feet with a wordless cry. Trubb and

one of the guards pinioned his arms and dragged him forward.

"Mam . . . ," he whispered.

She was too far away to hear him, but he knew that she heard anyway. She was looking at him, a smile on her lips and in her eyes, and he was smiling back at her. Even here, in the midst of this desperate struggle, just seeing his mother again made his heart feel like it was singing.

"Now, then," the Chancellor said as she returned to her place on the dais, "we can get started. There's work to be done here!" She smiled brightly at Raffa and then at Salima and Trixin. "The leadership of this pitiful collective—where are they?"

She scanned the crowd before her. None of the Afters moved. Raffa had not seen any of the council members other than Fitzer; he made a conscious effort not to move either his head or his eyes. He didn't want to inadvertently give any of them away.

"Really!" the Chancellor said. "You must not imagine that we are unjust or unfair. We only want what's best for Obsidia. None of the Afters will be punished for this insurrection. You will be allowed to leave with your families." She swept one arm through the air in a gesture of grand graciousness.

"But we must maintain the rule of law, for the safety and security of our citizens. We must deal with the leadership of this rebellion ruthlessly, to show that *no one* is above the law. No person may put their individual desires above the good of Obsidia."

Pause, while she surveyed the crowd again.

"Are they cowards, your leaders? Would they hide behind you—use you as human shields?"

Someone in the crowd stood, his hands raised above his head. He had long straight black hair tied back in a tail, dark eyes, and tan skin.

"My name is Sy," he said, in a strong, ringing voice. "I am head of the council here."

Raffa swallowed his gasp of surprise. He had never met this man, Sy.

He's lying, to protect the real council!

Raffa's heart filled with pride and admiration.

The Chancellor nodded. "So there *is* a true leader among you," she said, "one brave enough to take responsibility for his grievous error. Guards?"

Two guards made their way toward Sy. They took him by the arms, one on each side. Sy went limp and bent his knees, so he was hanging from their hands.

Raffa saw the Chancellor's face tighten in anger.

"You may delay justice, but you will not deny it!" she shouted.

"Take him yonder," she said to the guards as she pointed behind her, toward the stream. "And one of you come back—with his hand."

The crowd gasped; a few people cried out.

Raffa saw Elson and Quellin stand at the same time. Haddie and Missum Abdul and Fitzer stood, too.

"Ah," the Chancellor said, her face and voice smooth again. "At last, the truth. Won't you join us, please?" She beckoned them in a ghastly mock-welcome.

Soon there were nine people lined up in front of the dais: the five council members, Raffa, Salima, Trixin, and Sy. The other captives deliberately bumped into one another and their guards, creating a space of confusion that enabled Raffa to end up next to his mother.

Salima raised her bound hands over his head. He slipped under her arms. Since his own hands were bound as well, he could not hug her back, but he pressed his face against her shoulder and wished for that moment to last forever.

"You're taller," she murmured into his ear, "and that is the most dreadful haircut I have ever seen."

He had to laugh even as tears were rolling down his

cheeks. Several days earlier Jimble had given him a haircut, using Raffa's knife. Raffa had in fact not even seen the results himself—he hadn't wanted to.

"The Advocate?" he whispered.

The light in her eyes dimmed a little. "I don't know—"

Before she could finish what she was saying, guards yanked them apart and forced him to stand at the other end of the line.

"Nine . . . ," the Chancellor was saying. She strode down the length of the dais, passing each one in turn. "I realize that a few are missing, but this is very satisfactory, to have gathered most of you together so easily. Nine, to pay the price for the sins of hundreds—it's more than generous of us, don't you think?"

Pay the price? What does she mean by that?

"And as a further mark of our generosity, I hereby order that the executions be swift and merciful," the Chancellor said.

A wave of horror rolled over the crowd of Afters. Raffa could hear gasps and moans; some people began to sob.

"No," Haddie said, her voice firm. She raised her

hands to point at Raffa, then Trixin. "You'll not execute children. Not even you would be so cruel."

"Of course not," the Chancellor said. "Nor will I banish them with the others. I've decided that they will take up residence at the Garrison. For the rest of their lives."

Raffa had not even begun to take in the dread of what she had been saying when someone else spoke.

"Chancellor, your pardon?"

Raffa's head snapped in the direction of the voice. A voice he had known since the day he was born.

Uncle Ansel.

"I—I don't mean to speak out of turn," he said. He was clearly nervous, his eyes darting about, hands clasped but fingers fidgeting. "But I thought we—that is, earlier you and I spoke—that my sister might be spared . . . both she and my nephew could well be useful to us—"

The Chancellor stared at Ansel, obviously displeased with him. Her anger made her seem taller.

"I said I would consider your request, Senior Vale," she said. "I made you no promise. Do you recollect that now? Or are you calling me a liar?"

Ansel seemed to shrivel at her words. "Y-y-yes, Chancellor. No, of—of course not." He bowed his head in silence.

Then an anguished voice shattered the stillness. "DA!" Garith shouted. "Da, you can't still be with her!"

Ansel's head jerked up. Garith was standing at the edge of the pavilion. He stretched out one arm toward his father. Raffa watched as his cousin and uncle stared at each other.

Ansel put his face in his hands in utter dismay—but did not move from the Chancellor's side.

Garith held his arm out for a moment longer. It seemed to take forever for him to lower it to his side.

Raffa felt a corner of his heart break away, a wound that he knew would not heal. Uncle Ansel, whom he had loved like a second father. He would always love the man of his memories, but he could only pity the one here now, for the choices he had made and for being too weak to renounce them.

And as Raffa looked at Garith, he sensed that his beloved cousin would never be free from the pain of this moment.

CHAPTER THIRTY-TWO

TWO guards brought Garith to the dais and shoved him into the line of prisoners. Raffa saw that Garith's face was streaked with tears.

"Senior Jayney," the Chancellor said, "the six adult prisoners are to be taken one at a time to the stream, and executed as the captain of the guards sees fit. The others will remain in sight of everyone here, until it is their turn."

Some of the Afters could no longer contain themselves.

"Savagery!"

"Murder!"

"What about their right to be Deemed?"

The crowd was now simmering with restlessness. More angry voices filled the air. At that moment, with the guards and the Chancellor focused on the crowd, Raffa felt a familiar *whump* on his shoulder.

"*Echo!*" he whispered as quietly as he could. "Get under my tunic, quickly!"

The bat obeyed, but before he disappeared from sight, he squeaked out a few words.

"Not Mam horse," Echo said. "Da horse."

Da!

Da was on his way here! He had somehow escaped from the Garrison!

His heart nearly bursting from his chest, Raffa lowered his chin and spoke into his neckline. He had to find out if Da was bringing the Advocate with him.

"Echo, was there someone with Da? Another man?"

"Da horse," Echo repeated.

Raffa held his breath to keep from blubbering in distress. And fear, too: *The Advocate isn't with him. He mustn't come here! He'll be caught and executed along with the rest!*

"Man horse man horse," Echo chirped.

The world stopped. Raffa forced himself to speak calmly.

"What did you say, Echo?"

"Da horse. Man horse man horse."

Raffa closed his eyes for a long moment. He had never known Echo to count any higher than two.

Da, with at least two other people. The Advocate . . . But who else?

Callian!

Raffa opened his eyes. He craned his neck, looking down the line of prisoners at Salima. He saw her glance in the direction of the path into the clearing—not once, but twice.

She's looking for them! She's thinking—hoping— that they're going to get here at any moment!

But it was no longer a matter of the Advocate arriving in time to free the Afters.

Now it was a question of saving the lives of seven people.

Including Mam.

The noise from the crowd grew louder. The Chancellor stepped forward, her eyes narrowed. She raised a closed fist in the air over her head. All the guards immediately brandished their weapons.

The protests subsided, except for a murmur of voices in a far corner of the pavilion. Then a single voice was heard over the others.

"Hoy there! I need to speak to the Chancellor!"

Kuma!

Panic stampeded through Raffa's gut. *No no no— get away, get back to the Forest! They'll put you in the Garrison, too!* For someone like Kuma, who loved being outdoors and spent most of her life there, being locked up in the Garrison would be worse than dying.

The Chancellor looked up and out over the crowd. Kuma was hurrying through the clearing toward the pavilion. Two guards rushed to meet her; she raised her hands above her head and continued to walk toward the dais.

She stopped within arm's length of the Chancellor, her back straight, her body steady.

"Roo is somewhere out there, in the trees," she said. "All I have to do is call her, and she will come to my aid. She will rip and claw and tear anyone she thinks is hurting me. And look where I am—standing right next to you."

Raffa couldn't believe his ears. Kuma was threatening to use Roo as a weapon, the very thing she had sworn never to do!

The Chancellor went very still. "The bear would never get to me," she said. "My guards would lance it on sight."

Kuma lifted her chin. "You've seen her. You know how big she is. She could take a dozen lancers before she went down, and I doubt you have a dozen guards brave enough to face her. If she thinks I'm in danger, nothing in the world will stop her."

The Chancellor hesitated.

Kuma went on, "Let them go"—she gestured to the nine captives—"and order your guards to put their weapons down."

Chancellor Leeds pressed her lips together for a moment. Then— "Guards!" she shouted. "Silence her!"

Kuma responded calmly as a javelancer was thrust dangerously near her face. "I wouldn't do that," she said. "I don't actually need to make a single sound. Roo can smell me—she can even smell my fear. If I'm in distress, she will know it in an instant."

The Chancellor turned to Jayney. "Have some of the guards defend against the bear," she ordered.

Jayney seemed to falter for the merest moment, then turned to look out at the guards, who stood menacingly over the Afters seated on the ground. Every last guard suddenly focused on their charges, prodding the Afters with their weapons or barking orders. Raffa snorted in derision: It was obvious that not one of them wanted to be chosen to face Roo.

"One from each platoon!" Jayney shouted.

The guards only increased their efforts to look occupied.

Jayney took a step forward and raised his lancer. "Platoon leaders! Choose someone *now*, or come forward yourself!"

More shouts followed. The platoon leaders issued orders, but had to resort to threats and coercion before any of the guards would obey. Both Jayney and the Chancellor looked furious.

Finally fifteen men and women took up defensive positions around the dais. They muttered amongst themselves, plainly unhappy—and afraid.

They're not with her, Raffa thought. *They're following orders because it's their job—not because they believe in what she's doing. Most of them, anyway.*

The Chancellor sneered at Kuma. "Go ahead," she

said. "Let us hear you scream."

Raffa's eyes widened as he stared at Kuma. She opened her mouth . . . for what seemed like a very long moment.

But no sound came out.

Slowly she closed her mouth as she lowered her head. *She can't do it. She was bluffing.* He let out his breath; he hadn't realized he'd been holding it. For a moment, he couldn't decide if he was dismayed or relieved. Then she looked at him, and he gave her a firm nod.

It's okay, Kuma. You did the right thing.

A smile spread across the Chancellor's face. Again, Raffa was struck by how . . . how *normal* she looked. *If I didn't know what I know, I would have said that she has a nice smile.*

"Apparently we are going to be able to proceed without interruption," she said. "Guards, please see that our latest guest is properly welcomed."

A guard tied Kuma's hands and forced her into the line of prisoners.

"At last we're ready," the Chancellor said. Her gaze raked over the prisoners, now ten of them. Then she looked again at Salima.

"You"—she nodded—"you will serve as our first example, as your act of treason is the gravest. It is one thing to commit a crime. It is another to betray those who have trusted you. Guards?"

Two guards grabbed Salima by the arms. She folded her body limply, which angered one of them.

"Filthy wobbler," the guard said. He struck Salima across her back with the shaft of his lancer.

Raffa cried out at the crack of wood on flesh. He couldn't see his mother; she was at the other end of the dais.

"I'm all right, Raffa," Salima called to him, her voice steady upon solid.

They're going to execute her. They're going . . . to KILL her.

Raffa's stomach roiled in such fear that the foul, burning taste of bile rose in his throat. He swallowed, almost gagging.

Where was the Advocate? If Echo had seen him, it meant he was on this side of the river. How much longer before he arrived?

"Captain, what is the matter with your charges?" the Chancellor demanded. "Are they always so slow to respond to orders?"

The guards had pulled Salima forward, so now Raffa could see her. She was looking at him, her eyes on his face as if she were holding him, as if she would never let go.

He wanted to shriek and wail and bawl like an infant. He tightened every muscle in his body to stop himself.

Crying won't help her! Think—THINK!

How could he distract the Chancellor? It would have to be something big, something that would totally command her attention. . . .

Then it came to him.

"CHANCELLOR LEEDS!"

CHAPTER THIRTY-THREE

THE voice was so shrill that Raffa hardly recognized it as his own. He had spoken immediately—before he could think anymore, before he could change his mind.

Every head turned in his direction, including the Chancellor's.

He walked toward her, stopping just a few paces away. With his bound hands, he reached for his neckline. Awkwardly, he pulled out the perch necklace and held it up. Echo hung from the twig, asleep, but twitching now from the disturbance.

"This is the bat you want," Raffa said, "the one that talks."

The Chancellor frowned. "You and your friends are not known for truth-telling," she said. "How do I know you're not trying to deceive me? That could be any bat."

The pavilion was utterly, eerily silent.

Raffa blew a puff of air at Echo's whiskers. "Echo," he said gently. "I know it's your time for sleep. But I need to talk to you."

"Raffa talk," the bat said grumpily. "Echo sleep."

Gasps and excited whispers from those near enough to hear. Some people leaned closer in fascination; others drew back in fear.

Tears had begun streaming down Raffa's face.

I'm sorry, Echo. I'm so so sorry. . . .

Echo didn't know it, but Raffa was betraying him: Everyone would now know for certain that the little bat could speak.

Echo would never again be safe among humans.

"How amusing," the Chancellor said. She sounded ironic, her voice dry and detached. But she could not hide the gleam of surprise and interest in her eyes.

Echo stretched his wings sleepily. He blinked a

few times, then looked around and saw that they were surrounded by other people. He clicked several times rapidly, a sign that he was concerned or annoyed.

"What is it, Echo?" Raffa asked.

"People many," Echo replied. "Don't talk."

The Chancellor could no longer disguise her excitement. She held out her hand toward Raffa.

"FORTY."

Raffa turned in surprise. It was Trixin who had spoken. Loudly.

"Forty, isn't it?" she said, addressing the Chancellor. "Forty-coin reward—that's what you said, for anyone bringing you the bat. Raffa, if I were you, I wouldn't give her a thing until she comes through with the coin."

Trixin went on, speaking faster now. "Forty coin—you must really want that bat! And Raffa, what will you do with the money? I've never seen forty coin all at once. I wouldn't know what to do with it. I'd have to make a list. Boots for the little ones, for a start—they grow out of them so fast, and they're so expensive. I'd get them in every size for Brid and the twins. And Jimble, too—he's still small, but I expect he'll start growing like a weed soon, the way most boys do—"

What is she talking about? Boots?!

"—as for myself, this will probably sound, oh, I don't know, silly or vain or something, but I'd love a lockbox. To put my things where no one else could get to them. I'm forever searching for my hairbrush or for pins or my headscarf. I expect you don't have to worry about that, Chancellor—your servients probably know where everything is and all you have to do is snap your fingers—"

Then Raffa realized what she was doing. *She's stalling! She must know that the Advocate is on his way, too!*

A few of the guards tittered. The Chancellor's face twisted in fury.

"Is there no end to your impertinence?" she shouted at Trixin. "Guard, gag her!"

"Oh, there's no need for that," Trixin said. "I'm done. For now, anyway."

Raffa was amazed at Trixin's steadiness. She sounded as if she were having a perfectly ordinary conversation.

"Give me that bat," the Chancellor snarled.

Raffa moved slowly. His plan had been to use Echo to distract the Chancellor long enough for the Advocate to arrive, and then to tell Echo to fly away. But the Advocate had not yet appeared—which meant that Raffa would have to buy more time by handing Echo over to the Chancellor.

His muscles seemed to have frozen in anguish. His hands were still tied together; he had to use his thumbs to lift the leather cord over his head.

The Chancellor could wait no longer; she reached forward and snatched the perch necklace away from him. Raffa cried out; it felt as though she had torn off his arm.

She held the necklace up, with Echo at her eye level. "So, bat," she said, "your first words to a Chancellor . . . What will they be?"

Echo gazed at her steadily but said nothing.

She gave the perch an impatient shake. Echo swayed but remained silent.

"What's the matter with it?" she demanded. "Why won't it speak?"

Raffa restrained his impulse to cheer wildly. *He's not going to talk until he hears me say the word* friend. *Echo, you clever, wonderful bat!*

"He—he only talks when he wants to," Raffa said. Which was absolutely true.

Then Echo fluttered off the perch and landed on Raffa's arm.

"Seize the creature!" the Chancellor said to Jayney.

Jayney looked startled at first, then irritated; it seemed he thought the task beneath him. "Trubb, get that bat," he said.

Trubb winced and recoiled. "Don't like bats," he said. "Them claws—all scrabbly. And pointy little teeth." He turned to the guard beside him. "You take it."

The guard drew back. "Senior Jayney told *you* to take it."

Trubb sniffed. "I outrank you, and I'm ordering YOU to take it."

"*Outrank me?* You're not a guard—you don't even have a rank."

Raffa seized the chance before him. He rubbed his chin on the top of Echo's sweet furry head.

"Go, Echo," he whispered fiercely. "Go *now.*"

Echo launched himself off Raffa's arm.

The Chancellor shrieked, "It's escaping!"

In a panic, two guards swung their pikers wildly at Echo. One blade came within a hand's-width of the Chancellor's nose.

"Fool!" she shrieked, leaping back.

"Go, Echo, go!" Raffa shouted.

"RAFFA!"

He whirled around in joy and disbelief. "DA!"

Three horses and their riders burst into the clearing. Raffa saw his father, Mohan, at the fore, with Callian and Advocate Marshall behind him. They reined to a stop near the rear of the dais, between the pavilion and the stream.

Raffa's legs nearly collapsed under him. They had done it! All the desperate ploys by Kuma and Trixin and Raffa himself had given the Advocate and his escorts time to reach the clearing. He saw that the Advocate's face was thin and haggard, but his eyes were bright with purpose.

The Advocate stood in the stirrups.

"GUARDS!" he called out, his voice strong and clear. "You are under my command—mine, and no one else's. Draw down your arms at once!"

"NO!" the Chancellor shouted. "REMAIN AT ARMS! The Advocate is no longer competent to lead you! I command you now!"

"She has held me captive these past months," Advocate Marshall said. "Dosed with harmful apothecary and imprisoned in my quarters."

Raffa was close enough to see Chancellor Leeds press her lips together in an effort to maintain her composure.

"He *lies*," she said. "He can no longer tell truth from reality! See for yourself how unwell he looks!"

Heads turned back and forth between the Advocate and the Chancellor. Some guards lowered their arms; others continued to wield them. No one else moved. The silence was so tense that Raffa felt like the very air might explode.

"Proof!" From the crowd in the pavilion, one of the guards spoke up. "Advocate Marshall, can you *prove* that she's done what you say?"

The Advocate held out his right arm and pushed up his sleeve. A guard nearby stepped forward; Raffa could not see what the Advocate was showing her.

"Secure him immediately!" the Chancellor shouted.

The guard turned to face not the Chancellor but the crowd in the pavilion. "Hoy!" she called out. "The Advocate has deep wounds on his arm, both old and new. They are wounds from being bound by manacles.

I consider this adequate proof that he has indeed been held a prisoner!"

A rumble of voices quickly grew into a roar from both Afters and guards.

"She locked him up?"

"He's the Advocate! How did she dare—"

"She lied to us!"

Guards everywhere drew down their arms. They filed away from their captives and started forming up in platoons around the edge of the pavilion. The guard nearest Raffa cut loose his bonds; all the prisoners' hands were freed.

Raffa was left blinking in astonishment.

CHAPTER THIRTY-FOUR

WAS *that real? Or did I imagine it?* He rubbed his wrists, chafed from the bonds. *My hands aren't tied anymore—it really did happen!*

The riders dismounted. The Advocate stepped onto the dais.

"Chancellor Leeds, Senior Jayney, Mannum Trubb," he said. "You are under arrest for treason, and I am quite certain we will find ample evidence of other crimes as well. Guards, please restrain them."

Before the guards could react, the Chancellor ran off the dais and flung herself onto the nearest horse. It was Callian's horse, Mal. She yanked on the reins and dug her heels into the horse's flanks.

The horse did not move.

"HI-UP!" the Chancellor screeched, and lashed at the horse with the reins.

The horse tossed its head and stamped in annoyance—but otherwise didn't budge.

"Good, Mal," Callian said. "Good horse." He glared at the Chancellor. "He obeys only me. Dismount now, or I'll tell him to buck you off."

Three guards stepped up to the horse. One of them reached toward the Chancellor.

"Don't you dare touch me!" she shrieked. From her seat atop the horse, she turned and looked out at the crowd, Afters and guards alike.

"Do none of you understand?" she cried out. "I love Obsidia! I did what I did out of loyalty to this land! I used the animals so that guards would not die, your daughters and sons, your husbands and wives—everything I did was for the people's good! We are better off without the slum dwellers—surely you can all see that!"

In the silence that followed, Raffa was struck by a realization. *She really believes what she's saying. Which means that she's . . . small-minded. And small-hearted*

*as well—too small-hearted to care about anyone who's
not like her.*

"Guards, take her," the Advocate ordered.

"Don't touch me!" she said again.

She slid off the horse. As two guards took her by
the arms, Jayney moved more quickly than Raffa could
think.

He found himself in a chokehold, Jayney's heavy
forearm across his throat. Instinctively he raised his
hands, struggling for air.

Then he looked down and saw the glint of a knife in
Jayney's other hand, the blade pressed against his ribs.

"RAFFA!" Salima screamed. She lunged forward,
trying to reach him. She lost her balance and fell against
Trixin.

"Release the Chancellor," Jayney said to the Advocate. "Or the boy dies."

Raffa could not speak, could not breathe. Panic
spread through his body. He beat his hands uselessly
against Jayney's arm.

The guards who had taken charge of the Chancellor
looked at the Advocate questioningly.

"Let her go," the Advocate said.

Freed, Chancellor Leeds hurried to stand behind Jayney, who still had firm hold of Raffa. He eased the pressure on Raffa's throat just enough to allow for a quick breath. Jayney began walking backwards toward the edge of the dais, dragging Raffa with him.

"Let him go!" Salima cried out. "You have the Chancellor. *Let him go!*"

Jayney ignored her. He jerked his chin at the Advocate. "We are going to ride off now," he snapped. "If you follow us, I will kill the boy. Once we're safely away, I'll leave him off somewhere."

Mohan was staring straight at Raffa. Raffa stared back in fear and desperation. Mohan raised his fist to his mouth, biting his knuckle in a gesture of sheer anxiety.

Even in his state of terror, Raffa found that he was still able to think. *Odd . . . I've never seen Da do that before, bite his fist like that—*

Then he knew.

He's signaling me!

Raffa turned his head toward Jayney's shoulder. He opened his mouth and bit down with all his might, so hard that he felt flesh tearing beneath his teeth.

Jayney screamed in pain and loosened his grip. Raffa ducked and slipped out of his grasp; he fell, hitting his head on the edge of the dais. Sparks whirled in his vision. He heard a tumult of shouts and boots thudding—

"Guards!"

"Someone—quick—"

"No, DON'T! He has a knife!"

"MOHAN! NO!"

The last was Salima's voice.

Raffa's brain jangled with pain; he had to hold his breath to keep from vomiting. *Da! I have to help him....*

It took him three attempts to get to his hands and knees. He began crawling to the edge of the dais as Salima threw herself down next to him. "Are you all right?" she asked urgently.

He nodded, then held out his hand. She hauled him to his feet and helped him step down off the dais.

Jayney lay on the ground. He was groaning and just beginning to stir; it was clear that he had been momentarily knocked unconscious. Guards rushed to restrain him.

A small group of Afters and guards were clustered nearby. They stepped out of the way as Raffa and Salima approached.

Mohan was sitting partway up, holding one hand to his head. Blood streamed from under his hand.

"Da!" Raffa cried out.

Mohan shook his head. "I'm all right," he said. "Salima, quickly."

He jerked his chin to the left, where another man lay sprawled with his face in the dirt. Two Afters squatted next to him.

Salima hurried to the man's side. Raffa followed her and was just in time to see her roll the man gently onto his back. The entire front of his tunic was soaked in blood.

"Mannum Fitzer!" Raffa cried out.

He fell to his knees next to Fitzer. One of the Afters handed Salima a knife. She sliced open Fitzer's tunic. The hilt of Jayney's knife protruded from Fitzer's belly. Salima's hands moved quickly, but the blood continued to spurt from the wound. Raffa glanced quickly at his mother's face—and saw only bleakness there.

Fitzer opened his eyes and looked right at Raffa.

"Hoy, young Santana," Fitzer whispered.

Raffa crept closer, his face wet with tears. "We did it, Mannum Fitzer," he said.

"We did," Fitzer wheezed in reply.

"We were—" Raffa was sobbing now. He wiped his eyes quickly. "We were a good team."

"None better."

Raffa leaned forward and kissed Fitzer on his cheek. On the skinstain.

"None better," Fitzer whispered again. He turned his head and gazed upward.

Raffa saw the sky reflected in his friend's eyes before they closed forever.

CHAPTER THIRTY-FIVE

"MANNUM Curiss Myers."

"Mannum Curiss Myers."

"Missum Willa Garcia."

"Missum Willa Garcia."

"Mannum Sherrum Lexin."

"Mannum Sherrum Lexin."

It was four days after the battle. Advocate Marshall was speaking at the Commons, in exactly the same place where the Chancellor had given her fateful speech. The Advocate had begun by honoring the battle's dead.

Raffa stood with his parents, listening as the shouters

echoed each name in turn. Two Afters had perished from wounds inflicted by the animals. Four guards had died when they tumbled into a hidden crevasse on the Mag. The council's strategy of surrendering in the clearing had doubtless saved hundreds of lives: There had been very little hand-to-hand combat.

Dozens of Afters and their allies had been injured by the animals, some of them seriously. And many animals had been killed when things had gone wrong—the collars had failed to burst, or people had panicked.

Advocate Marshall called out the last name.

"Mannum Decklin Fitzer."

"*Mannum Decklin Fitzer.*"

Tears spilled from Raffa's eyes yet again. He was crying a lot these days.

Tears of sorrow for Fitzer. Who had saved Raffa's life during the wolf attack, then saved Mohan's, too. Jayney had been trying to stab Mohan when Fitzer intervened, despite his injured arm, and took the blade himself.

Raffa recalled their first-ever encounter, when Fitzer had come to his aid as he tried to cross the river to enter Gilden. *Without knowing who I was—without even seeing me. I needed help, and he gave it.*

As simple as that.

Fitzer wasn't an After. But he was well aware of what it was like to be treated unfairly. In the too-short time that they had known each other, Fitzer had shown Raffa how to fight unfairness with both determination and decency.

It was hard to think of a more valuable legacy.

More tears of pain and loss, for Garith. Uncle Ansel was in the Garrison, awaiting trial, along with Jayney and Trubb and the Chancellor herself.

Garith had decided not to attend the speech. He and Trixin were with Jimble at the Commons infirmary.

Jimble had survived the wolf attack. He owed his life to Garith, who had stanched the bleeding, then cleaned the wound and plastered it with yellowroot leaves. But the bite had been so deep and ragged that Jimble's leg had to be amputated below the knee.

Thanks to a scarlet-vine poultice, Jimble's wound was healing quickly, and he was making a remarkable recovery. Although he was still in pain, his spirit was undeterred, and he had already begun experimenting with crutches. Salima, who was treating him, thought he might be able to go home in another few days. And

Raffa had reassured him that he could soon begin training as an apothecary.

"Did you ever know a one-legged pother?" Jimble asked anxiously.

Raffa shook his head. "No. But that just means you'll be the first."

Naturally, Jimble on crutches meant that the twins and little Brid had to have crutches as well. Their father, Mannum Marr, had made three more pairs of various sizes, despite Trixin's protests. "How will I even move about the house with all those crutches swinging around?" she had griped.

When Raffa first heard about the amputation of Jimble's leg, he had been overwhelmed by guilt. *It's my fault, for forgetting about the wolves. If I'd remembered—if we'd been better prepared—*

It reminded him of how he had felt when Garith became deaf.

Da noticed his despair. "Raffa, you made mistakes, it's true," he said. "Even so, you are not responsible for the actions of others."

He means the Chancellor, Raffa thought, and lifted his head a little. His next words came slowly. "Is there any way," he asked, "to make sure that your mistakes stay your own, and—and don't end up part of someone else's?"

Da shook his head. "I would have to consider that a yearning," he said. "People are a wonder. They will always surprise you, for both good and ill."

A pause. "What if we were to agree," Da went on, "that we might both work toward something like this: Think carefully first, and then act boldly."

"Both of us?" Raffa was startled.

Da raised his eyebrows. "Do you think me too old to learn something new?"

"No, I—" He'd actually never thought about it at all, the idea of his parents still learning.

He nodded, and Da nodded in return.

Now Raffa leaned against his mother. He inhaled deeply but quietly, filling himself with the scent of her presence, which helped slow his tears. Mohan's hand was on his shoulder, large and strong and warm.

"There is still much work to do," the Advocate was saying. "The conditions in the slums *are* a problem, an indignation. And there have always been those who would divide us—who would have us think more on our differences than on what we have in common, as

Obsidians and as human beings. It will not be easy, but we must never give up."

". . . *never give up*," echoed the shouters.

"I have taken the first step toward a more just society," the Advocate continued, "by naming three new Commoners. Haddie Oriole, Mohan Santana, and Quellin Woon—all of them Afters—will have full participation seats in the Commons until the next round of elections."

Mohan left Raffa's side to stand next to the Advocate along with Haddie and Quellin. The cheers and applause seemed to reach the sky.

More tears—this time, of pride and hope, for the Afters and for all Obsidians.

Salima hugged Raffa, and kissed the top of his head. She was crying, too.

It wasn't long before his eyes were dry: Somehow the crying never lasted as long when he had someone else to cry with.

"Friend!" Echo squeaked. "Friend friend, friend friend!"

He had just returned from his night feeding. Raffa was standing outside a tent on his family's land not far from the pother settlement. The tent would serve as a shelter while he and his parents rebuilt their home, which had been burned down on the Chancellor's orders months earlier.

A sizeable and interesting group was gathered there, a week after the Advocate's speech. Kuma kept an eye on Roo, who sat in the garden, with everyone else a respectful few paces away. Twig and Bando were trying to climb Jimble's crutches. Garith, Trixin, and Callian stood next to Raffa.

"Yes, Echo," Raffa replied. "All friends."

"Are we ready?" Trixin said, impatient as always.

Fitzer's wagon was hitched to two horses that could not have been more different in appearance. One was Callian's noble Mal; the other a much scruffier horse, old but sturdy. Raffa patted the older horse's neck.

"Here you go, Dobbles," he said, and gave the horse a piece of carrot.

Dobbles, his family's faithful cart horse, had vanished months earlier, after the cabin fire. He had been found in the Commons stables, probably commandeered by whoever had set the fire. So many things sundered by the Chancellor would never be whole again, but being reunited with Dobbles had been a small bright moment.

Callian sat on the wagon seat and drove, with Kuma

seated next to him. Everyone else rode in the wagon bed, except for Roo, who loped behind or beside, occasionally falling back but always catching up again.

They were headed for the gorge, on a sunny but brisk spring morning. Hepaticas and spring beauties bloomed lavender and palest pink in the ditches and verges. Callian drove the horses at a steady but leisurely pace, which enabled Roo to keep up and everyone else to enjoy the ride.

Trixin was talking about the picnic lunch she had brought.

"Crackerbread and cheese, of course. Dried apples and dried tomatoes. The Commons kitchen gave me a ginger cake *and* walnut cookies. Roseberry tea to drink. And guess what else?" She looked at everyone expectantly.

"Pickles and jams?" Raffa said.

Her face fell. "Jimble, did you tell? I'll skin you alive—I wanted it to be a surprise!"

"I didn't!" Jimble protested.

"He didn't—I was *kidding*!" Raffa said.

Everyone laughed except Trixin. "You won't laugh once you've tasted them. I brought rind pickle and cumber pickle and cappisum pickle, and bramble jam and apple fluff. Made them all myself last fall."

"Mmmm . . . prapple chab," Garith said. "I love prapple chab, it's better than good."

"Prapple what?" Trixin said, before she saw the sly grin on his face.

Raffa laughed again, in both delight and surprise. It was the first time he had heard Garith make a lipreading joke.

The picnic was not the main purpose of the trip. Raffa's friends were accompanying him as he took Echo back to the gorge. Roo and the raccoons would live in the Forest of Wonders, where all three had been born. Raffa knew that there would be many future visits to both gorge and Forest, with his friends, to his friends.

The magnificent cliffs rose on either side of the track. Raffa took a moment, and a breath.

The last time I was here, it was with him.

The gorge would always remind him of Fitzer. Other things would, too, like the river, where they had first met. Raffa already knew that at times sorrow would blind him when he least expected it.

But there were more memories. Compost. Egg-and-cheese turnovers. Frypans.

There would be smiles as well.

* * *

After lunch, after peaceful naps with full bellies, after games and mushroom-hunting, the sun began to fall and the gorge grew chillier.

Garith walked over to Raffa, who was sitting on a boulder, stroking a sleeping Echo.

"Now?" Garith asked.

"Almost," Raffa said. "Just a little longer."

He had talked things over with everyone several times. "I honestly don't think Twig will know the difference," Kuma had said. "It's mostly Roo she talks to, and that won't change."

"Bando never had very many words to begin with," Callian said. "I don't think he'll notice, either."

That left only Echo, who was now waking from his daylight sleep.

"Friends many!" Echo exclaimed, recognizing where he was.

"Yes, Echo, I've brought you back to the gorge," Raffa answered. "But I need to tell you something. It's not safe for you to talk anymore. Too many people know about it, and they might try to—to hurt you. So I've decided—"

Pause. Swallow.

"I'm going to make it so you can't talk. I'll come here to visit, and I hope . . . I hope you'll always remember me. But it will be safer for you if you can't talk, and—and you'll be like all the other bats again."

"Don't talk."

"That's right. Not even to me."

"Don't talk Raffa?" Echo tilted his head in what seemed to be puzzlement.

Another swallow. "I'll always talk to you, Echo. And you'll still be able to talk to me. Just . . . not with words."

Echo was quiet for a moment. Then, "Raffa good."

A sob and a chuckle at the same time. "Echo good."

Kuma and Callian approached, each carrying a raccoon.

Raffa took the small bag of antidote powder out of his rucksack. He held out the bag so the other two could each take a handful. Then he took some himself.

"I'll go first," Kuma said. Cradling Twig like a baby, she opened her fist directly above the raccoon's nose. The powder fell all over Twig's little face, into her eyes and mouth, too. She sneezed, then coughed, then trilled indignantly at Kuma.

"Sorry," Kuma said. She gave Twig a piece of dried

apple. Twig's delighted chirp showed that all was instantly forgiven.

"Our turn," Callian said.

He dusted Bando with powder the same way. But Bando had seen Kuma and Twig, and he knew what to do. First he put his hands over his eyes to protect them from the powder. And as soon as he was finished sneezing, he pawed at Callian, clearly asking for his own piece of dried apple.

Garith was watching Raffa closely. "Do you want help?"

Raffa was grateful for the offer, but he shook his head, not trusting himself to speak.

Do it quickly.

With one hand, he held up the perch necklace. Then he let the powder fall from his other hand onto Echo's wee face.

Echo coughed, then sneezed twice and shook himself all over. Raffa showed him a moonwing moth he had caught earlier, one of the bat's favorite treats.

Squeak squeak!

Echo made what was obviously a sound of delight. Raffa tossed the large moth into the air, and Echo left the perch to catch and eat it. Raffa's heart tightened into a hard knot as he gazed at Echo in flight. *The first time we ever talked, it was about insects . . . skeetos . . .*

Echo spiraled higher, then headed for the cliff face, where he would join the thousands of other bats that lived within the gorge's stone walls. Raffa watched until he could no longer see the little bat. Then he turned and was startled to see his friends staring at him, their faces full of concern. The knot in his heart began to loosen into something different—still sad, but fuller and warmer and softer.

"Time to go," Trixin said.

"You'll be back soon," Kuma said.

"Can I come then, too?" Jimble asked.

Garith said nothing, but reached out to put an arm around Raffa's shoulders. At the last second, he pulled his arm back and gave Raffa a mock gut-punch instead.

But Raffa had anticipated the trick and neatly slapped the punch away.

"Nice one," Garith said.

Raffa was about to reply when, to his surprise, Echo reappeared and swooped low one last time, squeaking and chirping and squeaking some more.

Raffa knew exactly what the bat was saying.

"I love you, too, Echo," he called as the bat flew away again.

For the rest of his life, Raffa would be able to close his eyes and see what he saw now: Echo's wings, criss-crossed by scars, glowing translucent against the sunfall sky.

Read Them All!

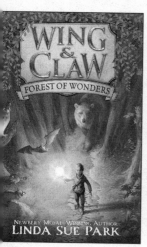  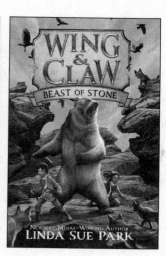

★ "With its engaging hero, talking animals,
arcane magic, moral issues, and unresolved plot,
[*Wing & Claw #1: Forest of Wonders*]
promises more exciting forest wonders."
—*Kirkus Reviews* (starred review)

HARPER
An Imprint of HarperCollins*Publishers*

www.harpercollinschildrens.com